Also by Will

OFF TI

FURTHER OF.

'Off The Mark' is a 'must read' for all ,   ..y-boomers', a diary of life growing up in sixties Norfolk invoking lots of memories, with plenty of jokes to get the wife asking what I'm laughing at! Had trouble putting it down, looking forward to the sequel...

'Off The Mark' is a funny, saucy portrait of life in sixties Norfolk, as seen through the eyes of Mark Barker, a wet-behind-the-ears school leaver in search of his first love. You get a real sense of time and place, with plenty of jokes to keep you chuckling along the way.

The book is easy to read as the writing flows smoothly and you very quickly find yourself drawn into Mark's world in a time more innocent than present day. What most impressed me was the depth the writer has gone into with getting to know the main character.

Tess of the Dormobiles

Will Stebbings

Printed by CreateSpace

Chapter 1

Theresa stared at her computer screen. It seemed to stare back at her, reminding her of those little staring competitions she had with Benny, her tabby cat. Theresa would often find Benny staring at her for no apparent reason, so she would just stare back until eventually the cat would weaken, blink and look away for a few seconds. This time, she had won again as her laptop slipped into 'sleep' mode. So she pressed a key to make it spring back into life, but still all that she could see on the screen was the title of her next novel – 'Tess of the Dormobiles'.

She felt a little guilty that she had stolen the title from Bob Richardson – a member of her former writers' group. As she knew that book titles couldn't be copyrighted, she had decided to go ahead and use it anyway, having first obtained Bob's blessing. Bob was the one person from the group to whom she felt she could talk. He had arrived at the group one evening and announced his plan for his next novel. It was to be about a young girl who had bought a campervan to go off for adventures in Dorset. Receiving no response from the group, he announced the title. When no one laughed, he just added 'Not really. It was just a joke; at least I thought it was.' Theresa was the only one who grinned, but that was the way of the group.

Bob's other little joke which she had enjoyed was when he turned up on his first night, telling everyone that he had just finished his first novel and was so pleased with himself, he was going back to the library to borrow another one. Again, Theresa was the only one to show any appreciation for his humour.

She had since stopped attending the writers' group as she

had found no help in obtaining a publishing deal for her previous novel. Theresa had imagined there might be someone there with contacts in the publishing world, but like all the writers' groups of which she knew, the attendees were all well-meaning amateurs. She realised that no successful writer or publisher would be interested in joining a writers' group. This group consisted mainly of elderly ladies who probably saw this as a social gathering. There were two members of the group who had published some unpaid articles in local magazines. Another person had seen a short story included in an anthology and one lady who had self-published a book of poetry – at considerable cost, it transpired.

Theresa didn't really understand poetry, although she had once read and enjoyed one of Spike Milligan's books. And she liked a good limerick. She remembered one that Danny had taught her –

There was a young fellow from Kent,
Whose tool was exceedingly bent.
So to save himself trouble,
He bent it up double,
But instead of coming, he went.

She couldn't quite remember the '*man from Nantucket*' but knew it wasn't as rude as it could have been. She could recall some of the words about the '*lady from Devizes, whose breasts were two different sizes,*' but she couldn't remember the rest of the rhyme, except that she thought that '*one of them won prizes*' or was she getting that mixed up with another limerick?

So back to this novel she was writing. Theresa didn't normally suffer from writer's block, but she was struggling to get this one started. Her original plan was to live the experience suggested by Bob, in that she would buy an old campervan and head off towards Dorset - until she found out that campervans were not a cheap form of transport. Those in good driveable condition attracted a sizeable purchase price.

Whilst she had traced two vehicles in her price range, they both needed a lot of work and financial outlay to make them even roadworthy, let alone make them reliable enough to go off on her own, although that might be an adventure in itself. Theresa was too fond of her home comforts to risk 'roughing it' so she abandoned the campervan option and considered using her Ford Focus to drive off into the sunset in the direction of Dorset. But then a friend and ex-colleague had offered the use of a small brick and flint cottage in Bircham St Mary in West Norfolk. The cottage was free for a few weeks, so that made more sense than heading off to the West Country and paying a lot of money for the privilege.

Theresa had sometimes been called Tess, but she didn't appreciate it very much. Some people also called her Treese, which she tolerated. However, she had decided that while she was in Norfolk, she would introduce herself to anyone she met as Tess, thus ensuring some authenticity to her experience – except that so far, she hadn't felt the need to introduce herself. She had spoken to a friendly lady in the village shop and said 'hello' to several locals who passed her in the street, but as yet, there had been no need to introduce herself to anyone. Even more importantly, there didn't seem to be any prospect of interesting adventures.

'So what do people do to make their lives adventurous?' she asked herself. For a start, Bircham St. Mary would not be their destination, so maybe she needed to venture further afield, but there may still be some interesting characters in the village and they might well hang out in the local pub. So she decided to pay a visit that evening. Meanwhile, she could at least try to get this novel started. After all, it was a great title and a great idea. *'Tess of the Dormobiles,'* she mouthed to herself. And then her mind started wandering again.

If this book was to be a success, she could expand the idea to other titles.

How about the story of a man, who owns a vineyard, which has suffered with bad harvests several years on the trot? So his future depends on one good summer to get him out of severe financial difficulty. It would be called *'Grape Expectations.'*

Or the story of a titled lady who had been ostracised by her peers because of her addiction to spreading gossip – *'Lady Loverly's Chatter.'*

Theresa's mind was working overtime now.

And then there's the adventure of the dashing rogue who has to steal some valuable gems to impress his heart's desire – *'Diamonds Are for Heather.'*

More titles flowed from her inventive mind – *'The Dirty Nine Steps;' 'A Womb with a View;' 'The Spy Who Came In With a Cold'; 'The Picnic Papers.'*

But still the screen stared back at her. None of this was helping her with her current work. Perhaps she was trying too hard. She pressed the 'save' button and closed her machine. She would have to eat before she ventured down to the pub.

She remembered visiting the pub about ten or eleven years earlier with Danny, her husband. In those days, they were still struggling to come to terms with their mortgage and could not afford holidays abroad, but Norfolk was an ideal location. As an architect still learning her trade, she had offered her services to her friend Judith who had bought this cottage in Bircham with the notion of turning it into a holiday let whilst also using it herself when she needed a short break. Theresa had helped design a small extension and convert one of the bedrooms into an en-suite. Because she was not at that time qualified, she performed the work for free. Theresa appreciated the opportunity to gain some valuable experience of that type of work, whilst she was still studying for her qualification. In return, Judith had told Theresa that she and Danny could use the cottage now and then when it was not being let.

Theresa loved Norfolk, particularly the small villages on the northern coast, with their creeks and salt marshes. She remembered their first stay in Bircham St Mary. When they visited the village pub, they had felt rather uncomfortable as the small number of locals stared at them as they entered the dingy looking bar. The landlord had been a little abrupt when they asked if the pub served food. But, yesterday, when Theresa had walked past the pub on her way back from the shop, she noticed signs outside advertising 'delicious local food' and the exterior had received a complete make-over, so she expected vast improvements. She couldn't imagine that the previous owner would have made much of a living as it was. Danny and Theresa had visited Norfolk several times since then, but had never felt tempted to re-visit the *Fox and Hounds.*

As Theresa prepared her meal which was to be a simple salad with thick juicy local ham from the village shop, she couldn't help thinking about Danny. She missed him so much. Their marriage had always seemed so solid and one based on honesty and trust. So to find out that Danny had been conducting an affair was devastating enough in itself, but to learn that it was with another man had totally destroyed any feelings of trust – and yet, she knew she still loved him. She was not anti-gay. She had friends both male and female who were gay and they were good friends. It was the shock of knowing that her husband had been leading a double life and had never felt he could confide in her. Now she felt that she had never really known him at all.

There had been no tell-tale signs. He had continued to enjoy all aspects of their marriage and always took particular pleasure in watching her dressing and undressing. It was true that he seemed more focussed on her bottom than any other part of her anatomy, but in her experience, that was pretty normal. And she was rather proud that her buttocks were still in good condition for a forty two year-old.

Theresa's first re-action when she discovered Danny's secret had been to tell him to leave and go and live with Arnold, but Danny refused as he still professed his innocence despite the evidence of the text messages. In any case, Arnold (Danny wouldn't reveal his real name) was married with three children. So it seemed that Arnold was also living a double life. And that was another thing. If Danny disputed the evidence, why did he refuse to reveal Arnold's identity? So much for honesty and trust in a marriage; although she begrudgingly respected Danny for keeping a confidence.

In the end, Theresa insisted that Danny should sleep in the spare room, but he found this unacceptable. If she wasn't prepared to trust him and listen to his protestations of innocence, he decided to go and live with his widowed father in Oundle. He believed that eventually, Theresa would see sense and this would all blow over.

Danny didn't really want the separation. Theresa didn't know what she wanted. Yes, she did. She wanted her old life back again and wished this had never happened – but it had. She couldn't imagine her life without Danny and at that moment she wished for a solution, but how could she ever trust him again? Wasn't her love enough for him?

They'd never been blessed with children. Danny had suffered with mumps in his teens, so there was a suspicion that he was sterile, but he refused to take any tests. He had old-fashioned views about masturbation, so wasn't prepared to provide a sample. Theresa's test had proved positive. In any case, they had both been too consumed in their careers to have felt regrets at the lack of a family, but now, Theresa felt it was fortunate that she did not have to explain all this to her offspring.

'Yes, dear; daddy still loves mummy, but he also loves a man.' Was she being too protective to think that would confuse a child? It certainly confused her. Theresa couldn't understand how anyone could love two people at the same time.

As usual, all these thoughts made her feel low, so she put on her favourite Grover Washington CD and sat down to eat her salad.

Chapter 2

Despite the lack of a breeze, it was turning decidedly chilly as Theresa ventured out through the dusk towards the pub. The scent of a forgotten and unseen bonfire invaded her senses, invoking so many memories of happier times. This period of the year when summer merged gently into autumn was normally Theresa's favourite time.

The house martins were gathering on the overhead wires, with their forked tails all neatly lined up. The swallows had already flown south for the winter. In the next few weeks, the autumn skies would be filled with the sights and sounds of the wildfowl heading for their feeding grounds among the salt marshes. Theresa always took pleasure in watching the chevrons of wild geese. She decided that while she was in Norfolk, she would visit one of the many RSPB centres dotted along the coast. She had heard that across North Norfolk, there were regular visits from egrets and marsh harriers, both of which could be seen in their winter roosts, although she wasn't expecting to stay in Bircham beyond the autumn.

The harvest moon was hanging over the horizon like a large coral pink ball. A spectral layer of mist was flooding one of the fields and a solitary tree seemed to be suspended in mid-air. This atmosphere led Theresa to conjure up images of dastardly deeds in Norfolk. She wondered if there were tales of smuggling in the vicinity; or perhaps some history of ghostly apparitions on the marshes, all of which could provide her with potential material for '*Tess of the Dormobiles.*'

It was with trepidation that she entered the '*Fox and Hounds,*' although it was now called '*The Bittern.*' 'Why do pub chains insist on renaming their establishments with new names, thus losing some of their tradition?' she wondered. One of the reasons for her trepidation was that she had been brought up to believe that ladies didn't enter bars unaccompanied. And then there was her memory of the last time she was in this pub, but she was pleased to see that the bar had received a make-over. It was no longer so dingy and the furniture was much more geared up for eating, although the olive green colour scheme was not to her taste. A few of the locals still stared at her as she walked in, but their attention was momentary.

'Hello, love. Are you eating with us, tonight?' the man at the bar asked. Theresa hated being called 'love,' but she showed no reaction. She thought that the speaker looked very much like the landlord they had encountered on their previous visit, but if it was him, he had lost his proclivity for bluntness.

'No, I've just come in for a drink. Can I have a cider, please?'

'Right you are, my beauty – one small cider coming up.'

'But I'd like a look at your menu, if I may. I might eat here another time.'

'Are you staying locally, then?' he asked.

'Yes, I'm renting a cottage in the village.' That wasn't strictly true, because Theresa wasn't paying any rent, but she felt there was no need to enter into such details.

'That would be *Cherry Tree Cottage*, then?' he enquired.

'Yes. How did you know?'

'There's only 2 holiday lets in this village and I've already met the other tenant. Are you just here for the week?'

'No, I'm here for a few weeks. I'm a writer, so I like to get away when I'm writing.' Theresa never wasted an opportunity to garner publicity for her work. She had self-published her first novel, which meant she had to do a lot of her own marketing. By mentioning her writing, she was hoping the landlord might purchase a copy of her book. She always carried some spare copies with her just for that purpose.

'You're not J.K. Rowland, are you?'

'You mean J.K. Rowling,' she corrected. 'No, I'm not. I wish I was. My name is Theresa Finbow. I don't suppose that rings a bell, does it?'

'Sorry, love. I never have time for reading.'

Just then, someone else entered the bar - a silver-haired thick-set man with a walking stick. He was probably in his late sixties, Theresa guessed. 'Hello Eddie, I'll be with you as soon as I've served this young lady. Are you on your own?'

'I am at t'moment. She's parkin' car.' The man had a Yorkshire accent. 'It's Pearl Harbour weather out there.'

'Come again?' the barman asked.

'Pearl Harbour weather. There's a nasty nip in the air' and then he chuckled to himself at his little non-PC joke.

As Theresa listened to this conversation, she was suddenly aware of eyes upon her. She turned to her right and there he was, sitting next to the window, staring at her. It was a look of pure malevolence and Theresa felt the hairs on her neck bristle – except that she didn't have any hairs on her neck. The owner of the stare was a red-faced man in his mid-twenties; possibly older. The kind of man you wouldn't take notice of if you passed him in the street, but now, Theresa was all too aware of him. Why was he staring at her? Did she know him? She didn't think so. She'd never done anything to anyone to cause such a hateful stare.

She took her drink and a menu and turned to find a seat. As she did so, she glanced over to the man again. He was still glaring at her. She deliberately chose a seat that was out of his line of sight, but it didn't stop her feeling very uneasy. Fortunately, the conversation between the landlord and Eddie was proving to be entertaining.

Eddie's wife had joined them and asked where her drink was.

'If you want a drink, you can order one,' Eddie said. 'You've got some money haven't you?'

'Are you telling me I've got to buy my own drinks, now?' the lady asked.

'Oh for God's sake get her a drink,' Eddie said begrudgingly.

'What will it be, Millie?' the landlord asked.

'I'll have a white wine, please.'

'So how was your holiday in Austria, Eddie?' the landlord asked whilst pouring a drink for Millie.

'It was good. The food was a little strange, though. One night, in t'hotel, they dished up this here sour krout stuff – basically cabbage in vinegar. It were horrible. I told the waiter that I couldn't eat it and asked if they knew how to cook cabbage proper, like. Well, he looked at me as though I were stupid.' Millie stifled a laugh and received a stern look in return.

'I told him that I didn't like to waste food, because everyone else on the tour was leaving theirs as well.'

'No, they weren't,' Millie interjected. 'There was only one silly sod leaving the food.'

Eddie decided to move on to his next complaint. 'When I ordered a beer with my meal, which weren't proper beer at all, it came with a head over an inch thick. I told him I wasn't paying for foam and that he should take it away and fill it up to the top of the glass. He came back and said he couldn't do that.'

'That's because he'd already poured you a full bottle and the beer was up to the little marker on the side of the glass,' Millie again interjected.

'Since when were you an expert on beer?'

'I'm not an expert on beer. I'm just an expert on common sense!'

'What about the holiday itself?' the landlord enquired in an attempt to stop them both bickering.

'Very pretty,' answered Millie.

'Everywhere we went in Salzburg,' interrupted Eddie, 'we

came across these women in burkas or whatever they're called. I'd like to have gone up to them and point out that there's nothing in the Koran that says that women have to wear burkas. I was very tempted except that they probably don't speak English.'

'So you've read the Koran, have you?' Millie asked.

'Have you?'

'I'm not the one who's trying to quote from it.'

'Do you two bicker like this, at home?' the landlord asked.

'No, he doesn't speak to me at home – which is the way I like it,' Millie said.

Theresa was enjoying this and wondered if she might use these two characters in her book. She decided to hang around for a while to see what else they came up with. This Millie was some kind of saint to be able to put up with Eddie who was an out-and-out grumpy old bigot – not unlike her grandfather, in fact, whom she had adored, but he was sadly no longer with them.

She studied her menu and decided there wasn't much to her taste. Everything was overpriced and the dishes, which were mostly seafood, were described in a very pretentious manner. What do they mean by *'temptingly accompanied by a sumptuous compote of spinach and chopped egg?'* Theresa was thinking she preferred good old British food like lasagne and chicken tikka – that was one of Danny's little jokes. If he had been there with her then, that's probably what he would have said – and she did wish he were there. There wasn't a day that went by when she didn't wish for his company.

After another look at the menu, she decided that she definitely didn't fancy eating on her own. She would have to make a trip to a supermarket to get more food to eat in the cottage. There was probably one in Hunstanton, which was the nearest decent size town. She finished her cider and returned the menu to the bar.

'Can I book you a table one night, love?' the landlord asked.

'No, thank you. I couldn't see anything to my taste.'

'We do have some specials every evening – over there on the blackboard.'

The specials didn't look particularly special. 'No, it's all right, thank you. I don't really like eating alone. Can I have a glass of red wine, please?'

Theresa could feel those eyes staring at her again. She decided she wasn't going to be intimidated by this weird person, so she turned to face him, intent on staring him down, but he had such a malevolent look about him that she relented. Instead, she whispered to the landlord. 'Is that fellow near the window one of your regulars?'

'That's Billy. Yes, he's often in here. Do you know him?'

'No, I've never seen him before in my life, but he seems to know me. He's been staring at me ever since I walked in.'

'I wouldn't take any notice of Billy. He's perfectly harmless.'

'Then why does he keep staring at me, like that?'

'He hasn't been the same since he was jilted about two years ago. It really hit him badly. He ended up losing his job on the farm because he kept making mistakes. You can't do that on a farm. I haven't seen him with a girl since.' Theresa could imagine him working on a farm. He looked weather-beaten and tough. He gripped his glass with stubby fingers and his hair was wild and tousled.

She decided to linger at the bar with her glass of wine and carried on listening to Eddie and Millie arguing. She started to plot their characters into her book. This was her second book. The previous one had been self-published and despite several good reviews, she had lost a small amount of money on it, but it had given her immense satisfaction that several people had told her how much they had enjoyed reading her work. Danny had been particularly supportive of her efforts and had sanctioned the expenditure. She didn't know if she could afford to self-publish this second book, but she was hoping the idea was so original that it might attract the interest of a publisher or literary agent.

Eddie was still in good voice. 'What has four legs and an arm?' he asked to anyone who was prepared to listen – not that anyone had a choice, his voice was so loud. Nobody offered an answer.

'A Rottweiler,' he announced.

'I don't get it,' said Millie. 'Why would a Rottweiler have an arm?'

'Because it's a Rottweiler. They're vicious animals that will rip your arm off if you're not careful.'

'That chap in Cleethorpes had a Rottweiler,' Millie said. 'And his dog was very well behaved.'

'It was just a joke,' Eddie said, holding his head in his hands. 'I don't know why I bother, sometimes.'

As there was an absence of diners, the landlord decided to join in the conversation. 'You do a bit of reading, Millie. This lady here is a writer. What was your name, love?'

'Theresa Finbow – call me Tess,' she replied remembering her plan to use her new name.

'Theresa Finbow,' repeated the landlord. 'Have you read any of her stuff?'

'I don't think so,' Millie replied. 'What have you written?'

'The last one is called *Happy is a Grumpy Road*. It's a little play on words after a song I heard by the Four Tops called *Happy is a Bumpy Road.*'

'What's it about?' Millie asked.

'It's about seven pounds,' Theresa replied, unable to resist repeating one of Danny's little quips. 'Sorry,' she added, remembering that she was talking to a potential customer. 'No, it's about this elderly chap who has been widowed for several years and is a self-confessed grumpy old man. Then one day he realises that he's got himself into a grumpy rut and seeks a soulmate. He tries dating websites and singles bars and meets a variety of ladies.'

14

'You know I met Millie at one of them singles bars, don't you?' Eddie said. 'You know, one of them places where lonely people go to meet someone of the opposite sex. It were quite embarrassing. I thought she were at home minding t'kids and she thought I were out playing darts.'

'Ignore him,' said Millie. 'Where would I find this book? Is it in the bookshops?'

'It might be. If not, you can ask them to order it. Or it's available as an e-book. But if you're really interested, I can let you have a copy, now. And I'll sign it, if you wish. I always carry a copy with me.' Theresa opened her handbag and fished out a pristine copy. 'It's had several good reviews if you look at my web-site.'

'It's a nice cover. What a lovely picture of the old boy. Is that the main character?'

'Yes, it's actually a picture of my grandfather. I used some of his experiences as part of the story. He died a few years ago and he was a lovely old chap. He always described himself as a grumpy old man, but he always made us laugh.'

'I'll have a copy. It sounds interesting. How many more have you written?'

'I've had one published and I'm working on my second at the moment. I hope you enjoy reading this – thank you.'

At that point, Eddie interrupted them to say 'Drink up! We need to get home to watch *Doc Martin.* It starts at nine o'clock.'

'I thought you were recording it?'

'I'd rather watch it live if we can. Come on!'

Theresa scribbled a message in the book and signed it. 'I'm here for a few weeks if you get chance to give me some feedback.'

As they both left, Theresa was aware that Billy was still unable to take his eyes off her, so she decided it was time to leave. The experience was already making her feel chilled, so when she stepped outside and discovered that the temperature had dropped several degrees since she had first left the cottage, she was starting to tremble. After a brisk few yards down the road, she heard the door to the pub close again. She turned to see that Billy was also leaving and walking in the same direction as her. It could just be a coincidence, but she wasn't hanging about to find out.

After a hundred yards, she could still feel his eyes bearing down on her. She didn't need to turn around to discover this – she knew. She walked as fast as she could without actually breaking into a trot. She could hear his footsteps and he seemed to be keeping pace with her. A quick look back confirmed that he was indeed matching her progress and now she was scared – really scared, but just then, another man appeared out of the mist in front of her. He was walking a dog; a small Scottie that barked as she approached.

'Hello,' she said to the walker, a middle-aged person smoking a pipe and appearing to be in no great hurry. 'I'm sorry to bother you, but that chap behind me is frightening me. He's followed me out of the pub and has been staring at me all night.'

'That's only Billy. He's harmless.' Why does everyone keep using the word *harmless*? 'He lives in this direction,' the man added. 'I'm sure he's not following you.'

That should have been re-assuring except that Billy had now slowed right down, whereas a few seconds earlier he had been hurrying to keep up with Theresa, who thanked the pipe-smoking gentleman and sped on her way, hoping to gain on Billy, but a minute after passing the dog-walker, he speeded up again and was gaining slightly. This was no longer a coincidence and it was with relief that Theresa reached her cottage. After fumbling in her bag for the door-key, she rushed in and bolted the door behind her.

It seemed to be pitch-black inside the cottage and Theresa leant against the front door panting. She preferred not to switch on a light and once her eyes had become accustomed to the darkness, she groped her way around to the front-room window to gaze out at the street, but the hedge obscured her view, so she crept up the stairs to look out of the landing window. Billy was standing on the opposite side of the road looking in the direction of the cottage, but after a few minutes, he moved off, presumably home to his house, wherever that was.

She sat down on the stairs still trembling, but taking deep breaths, determined to recover her composure. How she missed Danny. He would have tackled that idiot long before now.

There was a two-way switch for the lights on the stairs. She decided to edge towards the switch at the bottom, but her foot missed the step and her ankle gave way, forcing her towards the banister rail which she hit with her head, dislodging her spectacles. She heard them fall, but couldn't tell where they had landed. She wasn't badly hurt, but she needed her glasses to be able to see to find her glasses. She carefully felt each step with her hand as she moved down each one. She still hadn't found them by the time she reached the light switch.

But then she did find them – or rather her foot found them, with a snapping sound. 'Oh, no!' she said out loud. She immediately feared the worst, but when she picked them up, the frames and lenses were intact. However, one of the arms had snapped. It was a clean break and the only thing she could do was to hold the arm together with sticking plaster – not very elegant. She had a spare pair, but that was back at home. Who thinks to carry a spare pair of spectacles?

She could manage to see as long as she didn't move too much. That meant that walking was out of the question and so was driving. In any case, she didn't fancy being seen in public wearing spectacles held together with sticking plaster. She had to come up with a plan.

Chapter 3

Danny Whitehead put down his newspaper and let out a sigh. 'Are we going to watch *Doc Martin,* dad?' he asked.

'No, I want to watch this documentary,' his father replied.

'Can I watch it on the plus one channel afterwards?'

'As long as I can just see the news headlines first.'

'I wish you'd get satellite. Then we could record stuff. It would make life a lot easier for both of us.'

'I can't afford monthly rental. I've got to live off my pension, you know. If you don't like it, you can go back to your wife. I don't know what your problem is, you two, but you should sort it out. You're both miserable without each other. Why don't you ring her while I'm watching this programme instead of bothering me?'

'It's not as easy as that.'

It should have been as easy as that, but Danny knew that Theresa wasn't someone to respond to being hassled. If she were to ever forgive him, it would be when she was ready. He could try again to explain the text messages and tell her that he was no longer seeing Michael and he would tell her as soon as the opportunity arose, but he knew he had to do much more to regain her trust again.

He particularly wanted to watch *Doc Martin* because it made him laugh and he could lose himself for the best part of an hour and forget his misery, even though he knew it would return with a vengeance afterwards and keep him awake. He dearly missed her friendship; her warmth; her sense of humour; her laughter; her smile; her body, but most of all, he missed just being with her.

He looked at his mobile 'phone and wished that he could find a good reason to call her. And then the decision was taken away from him, because the 'phone did ring... and it was Theresa! He let it ring three times; not believing it was happening and trying to compose himself.

'Hello Fingles,' he said, but there was no reply and the 'phone went dead. Fingles was the nickname she had been given at school, as an affectionate version of her maiden name of Finbow, which she still used as her pen name. Danny had adopted the nickname and often used it in moments of intimacy. He particularly liked to joke that he wanted to visit Fingles' Cave and frequently described their foreplay as a Hebridean overture.

He wondered if he should call her back. Perhaps her 'phone was low on credit. That wasn't unusual for Theresa, despite his nagging. He left it a few minutes in case she tried again, but she didn't. So he went into the kitchen to call her back.

'Hello Danny,' she said. 'Can you hear me all right? I haven't got a very good signal. I'm in Norfolk. I'm after a very big favour. I've broken my glasses and my spare ones are at home. I can't go anywhere like this. Hello... are you still there?'

'Yes, but you keep breaking up. You've broken your glasses? Where are you if you're not at home?'

'I'm at Judith's place in Bircham. Is there any chance you could fetch my spare glasses? They're in the bureau in a brown case.'

'You want me to fetch your glasses to Bircham?' Danny was surprised that she would ask him to perform such a task.

'Yes, I know it's a long way, but I can't think what else to do. I can't go anywhere without them.'

'I'm not coming tonight.'

'Of course not. I wasn't expecting you to…just as soon as you can make it.'

'I've got to be at work tomorrow. I doubt whether I could get there before about seven o'clock and then I've got to drive

19

all the way back to Oundle. It's all going to be a bit of a rush.'
Danny knew he would gladly drop everything to see her, but
he didn't want to appear too eager.

'I didn't catch all of that, Danny. There is a spare bed here,
if it helps. Are you still there?' But the phone was dead again
and she could see that what little signal she had was gone.
Maybe she could get a better signal outside, but Billy could
still be lurking around. Norfolk was notorious for signal black
spots, so she was lucky to get through at all. She was just
hoping that Danny would turn up the next night.

Danny was trying not to get his hopes up, but at least his
feelings of despair could be put to one side. It was a comfort
to him that he was the person Theresa had felt to call. Of
course, he may not have been her first choice, but she had
called him, so she must have felt that there was still a place for
him in her life.

He called out to his father 'I'm making some hot
chocolate. Do you want a cup?'

'I can't hear you over the television,' came the reply, so
Danny went back into the lounge.

'I asked if you'd like a cup of hot chocolate.'

'No thanks. Was that Theresa you were talking to?'

'Yes. I don't know what time I'll be home tomorrow or
even if I'll be home at all.'

'Are you going over to Norfolk?'

'How did you know she was in Norfolk?'

'She told me last week. She often rings me up during the
day when she knows you're at work. She always asks how you
are.'

'And what do you tell her?'

'That you're a miserable sod and the two of you need to
sort out your problems – whatever they might be.'

'And what does she say to that?'

'She tells me that she can't talk about it to me – and you

won't talk about it, either, so I don't know why I have to put up with your miserable face. I can't bring my girlfriend 'round here when you're here to cramp my style.'

'Have you got a girlfriend, then?'

'I've got loads, but they're only after my body, so I have to pace myself. Can I watch this programme, now?'

The next day dragged for Danny. The situation reminded him of the day he got his very first date with a girl and in many ways, there was just as much chance of it all going wrong. He knew he just had to take this one opportunity to salvage his marriage.

Danny worked in Peterborough as an IT consultant. He had only been in his present role for eight months. His employer, WBL, was where he had met Michael. WBL was a relatively new company that had been formed when Danny's previous employer, Wilkinson Brewery had been bought out by the Boultons Hotel and Leisure Group.

Wilkinsons had been running as an independent brewery since 1946, concentrating initially on producing a single brew called *Wilkinsons Best*. This was particularly popular in the Fenland area and the farming villages of North Cambridgeshire where it had gained a strong reputation among the agricultural workers. As the company grew, it expanded its business by buying up local public houses and installing its own landlords. Wilkinsons were quick to get in on the bar-meals initiative of the seventies that saw many pubs tap into a new market. At that time, very few pubs would serve hot food, with such facilities being more aligned to hotels than to small bars.

Chicken in a basket was quite a novelty, as was *scampi and chips*. Danny remembered trying to order *soup in a basket* at the time and getting some puzzled looks. The bar-meals could be ordered by the casual visitor without having to book a table beforehand. By offering a very limited menu, Wilkinsons pubs were able to serve such fare almost 'on tap' with a pint of beer and this generated custom beyond their regular agricultural clientele.

The company's growth had been steady but reliable and the business had always been run as a family concern, treating its employees with particular care, thus promoting brand loyalty to customers and staff alike. They were one of the first pub chains to invest in *point of sale* devices to replace traditional tills and that was when Danny joined the company. By then, the head office had moved out of the Fens into a business park on the outskirts of Peterborough, which at that time was expanding rapidly. Danny was instrumental in implementing systems which enabled stock levels of all goods to be maintained at optimum levels in all pubs and buying trends could be monitored to ensure the right product ended up in the right location. He also introduced a system that allowed the pub managers, who had replaced the traditional pub landlord, to record staff attendance on the tills. Head Office could access these tills remotely to gather this data, thus facilitating quick and accurate calculations of payments to employees. Over the years, these systems became more and more sophisticated and guaranteed continued employment for Danny and his colleagues. During this period, the company added restaurant facilities to all its establishments as they struggled to combat the competition from cheap alcohol in supermarkets and this approach replaced the more casual bar-meals.

When Arthur Wilkinson retired, he entrusted the company to his two sons, who for a while, ran the business along the same lines as their father before them, but eventually, they floated the company on the stock exchange, feeling they needed greater investment to continue the growth of the business, as it was felt that to stand still really meant going backwards. That was when things started going wrong, because the investors became too greedy and wanted bigger

22

profits. This was at the time of the big 'dot.com' boom in the nineties when investors became accustomed to seeing big profits on their investments.

An approach by a team of venture capitalists gave the investors the opportunity to make a quick return on their investment. The venture capitalists installed their own top management, who started the process of asset stripping and closing less profitable pubs. Anybody who had worked for the company for more than ten years was viewed as being 'too comfortable' because in the views of the new management, anybody of any talent should be constantly looking for new opportunities. Thus the new owners chose to ignore the legacy that had brought Wilkinsons to such a prominent place in the leisure industry and rapidly destroyed the loyalty of the customer base. Redundancies were rife and morale suffered dramatically in a very short period of time.

Five of the new management team finished their 3-year contracts with six figure bonus payments on top of their lucrative salaries. The CEO received a seven digit sum. The turnover of the 'streamlined' company had by then halved, although selling some of the assets, including several of the less profitable pubs, had yielded some additional income.

'I could have screwed up the company for a fraction of that price,' Danny had argued to his few remaining colleagues.

Towards the end of that three year period, the chief executive negotiated a buy-out with Boultons. It was described in the media as a merger, but, in reality, Boultons had snaffled up a major competitor on the cheap. The new WBL brand was nearer to Boultons' image than Wilkinsons'. So a few investors had made a little extra money, but at the expense of dozens of employees who lost their livelihood. Some of those who had lost their jobs had moved on to better things, but many more were now living in reduced circumstances.

Danny was one of the survivors, but he never felt the same

motivation again. Then just two years ago, the new IT director decided to outsource all the IT services to an Indian company called VIS. This, it was alleged, would save the company two million pounds a year and provide the business with an improved IT service. The main concern of the IT staff was whether their jobs were at risk and at a team meeting, Danny and his colleagues put the question to their manager.

'No,' said the manager. 'Your jobs will be safe for at least two years while they conduct KT and they may then offer positions to some of you.'

'What's KT?' Danny asked.

'Knowledge transfer,' replied his manager with a disdainful look, as though everyone knew what KT was. 'It's quite a common thing in the IT industry.'

'Well, what does it mean?' Danny asked, not caring if everyone else knew what it was, but judging by the look on their faces, they didn't.

'You will transfer your knowledge to VIS staff and over a period of time, they will gradually assume your roles.'

'You mean you want us to train people to take our jobs away from us.'

'It's not as simple as that. It will be a timed and structured handover.'

'What if we refuse?' Sarah Turkington asked.

'You can't refuse,' was his answer.

'I can. I can look for another job.'

'Well, that's your call.'

'Why can't we just transfer to VIS?' Danny asked. 'That's what normally happens when companies outsource... and then we're covered by TUPE regulations.'

'Because VIS are based in India, so if they took you, you would have to relocate to India... and then there are problems with work permits, and so on. In any case, the deal they've put together is costed on using their existing staff.'

'In other words – cheap labour!' Sarah snapped.

'These people we're supposed to be training; are they based in India or will they be over here?' Danny asked, doing his best to contain his anger.

'I don't know all the answers at the moment, but certainly, the plan is that the help-desk will be based in India,' the manager replied.

After a few more fractious questions and comments, the meeting broke up to the sound of disgruntled murmurings about what each individual was going to do.

As they walked out, Sarah asked Danny what he was working on at that time. Danny replied 'My CV!'

'It's a good job you have a sense of humour,' Sarah said.

'Yes… a mate of mine has just lost his job at Alton Towers. He's taking them to a tribunal for funfair dismissal.'

Now, two years later, Danny was still employed at WBH, having reluctantly passed on a small amount of his knowledge, whilst retaining enough to stretch out his employment a little longer. Sarah had refused to participate in KT, but was fortunate enough to find a new job after only a few months and Danny was one of the few original Wilkinsons employees still working at WBL. The whole culture of the company had completely changed and this situation added to his personal misery.

Before being outsourced to VIS, Danny's work at WBL had taken him to various locations in the country, including the new company's head office in Norwich and that was where Michael had been based. Work on one particular project had meant they had needed to work closely together. Michael had paid frequent visits to Peterborough and Danny had reciprocated with visits to Norwich. It was on one such occasion in an hotel in Norwich when Michael had made his advances. Despite his appearances as a happily married man and father, this was not the first time that Michael had pursued a colleague in this fashion, as Danny was to discover only quite recently. Michael had the ability to exert a 'Svengali' influence over almost anyone who took his fancy and Danny hadn't realised until it was too late that he had been dragged into Michael's little world of luridness. The text messages meant nothing to Danny, but now served as incriminating evidence of something that wasn't entirely what it seemed. Danny still found it hard to believe that he had jeopardised his marriage by such foolishness, but with a bit of luck and a following wind that evening, he would be able to take steps to rectify the situation.

Meanwhile, he was required to spend an hour conducting some KT over the telephone with a 'colleague' in India – what fun!

Chapter 4

Theresa spent the day making a start on her novel. She would incorporate her experiences in the *'Bittern'* and expand upon the characters she had met, including Eddie, Millie and Billy. With each character she would exaggerate and embellish their behaviour. Eddie, in particular, became even more of a grumpy old bigot who thought political correctness, health and safety and all call centres were making the British way of life intolerable. Some of Eddie's fictitious views reflected her own, but in a way that put all the blame on Eddie (or Jim as he had become in the novel).

However, she would still set her book in Dorset. She wasn't sure if that was a good idea, because she really wanted to capture the atmosphere of that county, which she thought would be improved by personal experience. Perhaps, she would arrange to spend a few weeks there if her finances could stand it.

She decided that the character of Billy, now called Terry, would turn out to be a dangerous psychopath in her novel, which was going to be a thriller. Normally, at this stage in her writing, Theresa would have already mapped out a clear plan and structure, but she was still trying to do this, hoping that the next few weeks would give her additional inspiration.

Her first novel was claimed by some people to be semi-auto-biographical – something she vigorously disputed, whilst admitting some personal experiences had been included. She realised that with *Tess of the Dormobiles,* this was likely to be even more the case unless she added some events that could not possibly have occurred in her sheltered life.

As Danny couldn't sleep, he had risen early to make the trip to their home at Woodnewton before travelling on to his office in Peterborough. If he had waited until after work to call in at their house, he would have had to double-back along the A47. He found the spare spectacles where Theresa had told him to look. There was a small pile of mail that lay on the floor of their hallway, which Danny sifted through. It was mostly junk-mail, which he threw away, but there were a couple of things that looked more important, so he gathered them up to deliver to Theresa that evening.

He felt a chill as he looked around the lifeless hall-way and then the lounge. This was their little home which they had made together and now it didn't feel like a home at all.

Danny's job allowed a certain amount of flexible working, but he had a meeting that afternoon. He determined to leave for Norfolk just as soon as he could. This wouldn't allow him any chance to eat, but he intended to take Theresa out for a meal, so he made sure he was on the A47 by five o'clock.

It was a dreadful journey, which in Danny's experience was normal for the A47. He often felt that he would visit Norfolk more frequently if it wasn't for the tortuous journey and as much as he wanted to get there as soon as possible, he decided it would take as long as it would take. Overtaking would just move him up the queue a little further and would achieve very little – not that there were many overtaking opportunities; at least not until just after the end of the Wisbech bypass where he had a few miles of dual carriageway to assist his haste..

It was almost dark when Danny knocked at the door of the cottage. Theresa greeted him with a kiss on the cheek and a hug that lacked any real warmth. 'Thank you ever so much for doing this,' she said, swapping her spectacles and pulling a face while she got used to the replacement. 'I know how much you hate that journey. What were the roads like?'

'About the same as usual, but it was worth it to see you,'

he replied. 'How are you?' he asked as she ushered him into the cottage.

'I'm all right, thank you… and you?'

'You know how I am. Can we sort this silly business out?'

Theresa looked at him for a moment and then said 'Would you like a cup of tea?'

'Yes, please… and then we can sit down and have a talk.'

Theresa didn't respond to this and just disappeared into the kitchen. Danny followed her. It was several weeks since they had last spoken and they had so much to say to each other, but neither knew how to start.

Once the tea was in the pot, Theresa asked 'Have you eaten?'

'I just had a sandwich at lunch-time.'

'I haven't got much food in, I'm afraid. I had intended to drive over to Hunstanton to do some shopping, but I'm not going out with sticking plaster all over my glasses.'

'I noticed the pub as I drove past. They seem to do meals now. Would you like to join me, there?'

'You won't like the menu. I had a look last night. It's all overpriced fancy stuff – mostly seafood.' But then she thought that there wasn't much alternative unless they drove further afield so she added 'They do specials each night; so there might be something different tonight. I'll pay.'

They still kept a joint account so the offer meant nothing financially, but it meant an awful lot to Danny that she was making some sort of gesture.

By now, they were sitting down at the kitchen table with their cups of tea and again the conversation had faltered.

Danny felt it was time to grab the nettle. 'I'm going to tell you everything that happened with Arnold… and you will listen, please.'

Theresa bridled at this. She felt he was either going to tell her a load of lies or some graphic detail she didn't want to hear, but she did want their relationship to move on one way or another.

'This chap who exchanged texts with me… he works at the head office in Norwich and we had to work very closely together on a project. You may remember that I made several trips to Norwich. One night, he insisted that he entertained me in my hotel. We had a very pleasant evening meal with a bottle of red wine. I can't remember which sort, but it was one of those that you could just keep sipping. We were so busy talking that he hadn't realised that he had drunk much more than half the bottle and so couldn't drive home. He was going to get a taxi, but I told him that my room was a twin, so he could share the room. It was one of these hotels where the room rate was the same regardless of how many occupants there were and he could get a free breakfast out of it. I never meant anything other than sleeping in the second bed. He accepted – rather too readily I thought, but I didn't dwell on it. As we were both enjoying each other's company and he was no longer driving, we ordered a second bottle of wine and it was about one o'clock before we turned in.'

Theresa did not respond in any way. She wasn't enjoying any of this, because she could see this was revealing a side of Danny she didn't like. The Danny she knew wouldn't enjoy the company of another man in his hotel room.

'To cut a long story short,' Danny continued, 'he made a pass at me. He had totally misread the situation and I must have inadvertently given out the wrong signals. Anyway, I, of course, totally rejected his advances and told him he'd better leave. He apologised profusely and convinced me that it wouldn't look very good if someone saw him leaving my room at that time of the night. So he stayed. And there were no further incidents that night.

A couple of days later he started sending me texts – some of which you saw.'

'Yes,' Theresa said. 'He said he had enjoyed going to bed with you! What was I to think?'

'Well, you could have given me chance to explain, instead

of assuming the worst. That text was just his weird sense of humour.'

'Yes, but you responded that you had enjoyed it, too!'

'I was just going along with his silly joke. I've since found out that he has tried it on with other colleagues – male and female! And then, of course, to make matters worse, you saw his next text which said "love and kisses" - which I didn't respond to. I was going to just delete the texts but not before you picked up my 'phone and got…' Danny was going to say 'got all hysterical,' but he decided this would not have the desired effect.

'… and got the wrong idea,' he added calmly.

'I'm meant to believe all that, am I? Theresa asked. 'What didn't you mention this night in the hotel to me at the time?'

'For one thing, I suppose I felt a bit stupid about it… and because he'd asked me not to mention it to anyone.'

'Not even your wife?'

'I wish now that I had, but I was respecting a confidence. He is married and has got children, so I wouldn't want anything I said to risk all that – for their benefit, if not his. The next time I worked in Norwich, I made sure I didn't have to stay overnight, if you remember.'

'Yes, I do remember, now that you mention it.'

They looked at each other for a minute – Danny hoping that he had now explained the situation and Theresa considering whether there were still unanswered questions.

Danny spoke first. 'It's amazing that this is the first time you've actually let me explain it all. How could you ever think that I would ever be unfaithful to you in any way?'

'I didn't… that is to say… oh, I don't know. I suddenly wondered if I ever really knew you if you could go off and sleep with another man.'

'Well, I didn't – and I wouldn't… and you should have known that.'

'Of course I did,' she said biting her lip and looking as

though she were about to burst into tears.

'Anyway,' Danny said. 'What are you doing in Norfolk?' He felt if he changed the subject it would look as though they were getting back to normal.

Theresa looked a little surprise at this new approach, but answered anyway. 'I'm working on my next novel. I'm looking for inspiration and some time alone.'

'How long are you staying?'

'I can stay until the half-term holiday. Judith has already rented the cottage to someone else then.'

'What about your job?'

'I've got some holiday owing to me and I might take some unpaid leave. Things are very quiet at work, but there is talk of a project for some new housing at Hampton, so I may have to return earlier.'

'Shall we go and see what this pub food is like?' Danny asked. 'They might not take orders much longer. By the way, I've sold a couple of your books.'

'Who to?'

'One to my new Indian manager – he probably thinks it will improve his English. The other… I sold to Arnold. I haven't had any feedback from either of them, yet. And here's some mail I picked up from the house. Is that one a royalty statement?'

'Yes,' she replied while opening it. 'Thirty four pound twenty-five pence! Look at all these deductions. It seems everybody's making money out of my book except me!'

Danny said 'We really ought to get down the pub or we'll be too late.'

Chapter 5

It was dark as they walked down to '*The Bittern*' and the street lights were sporadic. In places the footpath came to an abrupt end so they had to venture onto the road. There was still a 'nasty nip in the air.' Danny wanted to put his arms around Theresa's shoulder to keep her warm, but he still wasn't sure if this would be welcomed. Instead, he reached for her hand. Theresa allowed him to hold it, but her hand felt stiff and he was aware that although he was holding her hand, she wasn't holding his. When a shrub impeded their progress and they had to separate, Danny didn't bother to try again.

The pub was busier than the previous evening and Theresa was pleased to see that Eddie and Millie were occupying the same position at the bar. The host greeted them with a smile and said 'Hello Tess. Good evening sir. What can I get you?'

Danny replied first. 'Are we too late to get some food?'

'We're a bit busy at the moment, but one couple has just requested their bill, so if you don't mind holding on for fifteen minutes, I'm sure we can accommodate you. Would you like a drink while you're waiting?'

Danny ordered their drinks and took a menu to peruse.

Meanwhile, Eddie called out 'Good evening, Tess.' Danny gave him a quick stare. He didn't like all these people calling his wife 'Tess.'

'Hello Eddie. Hello Millie,' Theresa replied.

'Hello Tess,' said Millie. 'Are you going to try our local fare?'

'Yes. Danny – my husband, here – is paying a quick visit, so we thought we'd eat out together.'

'When are you two going to sample our delights?' the landlord asked of Eddie and Millie.

Eddie replied. 'I married a perfectly good cook. She can match anything you can produce – and a lot cheaper, too. Whenever, I used to come home from work, she would always have something delicious waiting for me on the kitchen table. Then we'd have some food.' He was pleased with his little witticism and laughed longer and louder than his audience.

'He's all talk,' said Millie. 'His mate told me that before we met, he used to try and date girls who had asthma, because he thought they sounded as though they were enjoying themselves more.'

Eddie didn't seem to take any notice of what Millie was saying and he changed the subject almost before she had finished her sentence.

'So is this Mr Finbow?' he asked of Theresa.

'This is my husband, but it's not Finbow. That's my pen name. Our married name is Whitehead. This is Danny.'

'Pleased to meet you,' said Eddie and before anyone else could speak, he added 'I picked up your book last night. I don't do much reading, but Millie's still reading another one and I was intrigued by the title and about this grumpy old man. I think we all identify with that when we get to a certain age.'

'Eddie's been particularly grumpy since the doctor told him to pack up smoking,' said Millie.

'How long ago was that?' Theresa asked.

'About thirty years ago,' Millie replied and everyone but Eddie laughed. It seems that he only laughed at his own jokes.

'I've read the book,' came a voice from the corner – a voice with a very strong Norfolk accent. Theresa thought it was a woman's voice at first, because it seemed too high-pitched for a man. It was Billy, who had remained almost out of sight up until that point.

Theresa had momentarily forgotten about Billy and had not noticed him in the corner, surrounded as she was by so many people, but now the memories of the previous evening came flooding back. However, Billy's voice did not sound in the least bit menacing. You might almost say '*harmless*.'

Theresa was always interested in how people discovered her novel – a knowledge she felt might help her pitching her next book to bookshops or the media. So, although she still felt apprehension after her first encounter with Billy, she felt emboldened to ask him 'What made you buy it?'

And there was that worrying stare again. 'I didn't buy it. I borrowed it off my brother.'

'How did your brother come to buy it?'

He didn't answer straight away, but after a few seconds, he said 'He sold it to him' and pointed to Danny.

Danny looked a little puzzled. He asked 'Who would that be?'

'Michael… Bingham.' His stare was now upon Danny to gauge his reaction.

Theresa was also interested in Danny's reaction, because she always wanted to know who had bought her books, but now she wanted to know why Danny had turned white.

Danny recovered his composure and said 'You must be Carl?'

'That's right.' And still that unerring stare.

Theresa said 'I thought your name is Billy?' She realised after she said it that this would indicate to Billy that she'd been discussing him behind his back, but it was too late.

'My real name is Carl. People call me Billy after that footballer.'

'Billy Bingham,' said Danny. 'He managed Northern Ireland.'

Before they could continue the conversation, the landlord interrupted. 'Excuse me, sir. Your table is ready. Are you ready to order?'

They weren't ready to order. They'd been too busy talking, but Danny was hungry. 'Oh, I'll have the sea bass,' said Danny.

Theresa gave the menu a quick glance and said 'I'll have

the smoked salmon, please. We won't bother with starters.' She resented the fact that the Landlord had addressed all his questions to Danny – presumably because he was the husband and she was merely the little wife.

A waitress showed them to their table.

Once seated, Theresa wanted to know why Danny had turned pale, when Michael's name had been mentioned. When Danny hesitated, she said 'It's him, isn't it? The man you went to bed with. So he did mean something to you.'

'I didn't go to bed with him, as I've already explained. We slept in separate single beds.' Danny's teeth were grinding together as he said this.

'So why did you go so pale?'

'It was Carl. I told you that Arnold – Michael - had a lot to drink that night. He was doing a lot of the talking. Well, after a while, he started telling me all about an incident with his brother. I don't think he would have told me so much when he was sober. There was this girl and they were engaged to be married.'

'Yes, she jilted him,' Theresa said.

'Have you already heard the story?'

'No, I just heard that she had jilted him and he had taken it very badly.'

'Well, there's a lot more to it than that. Did you know she died?'

'No!' Theresa gasped as she heard that news. 'How?'

'She died due to a blow to her head. She may have banged her head on a low beam in her house, but Carl was taken in for questioning, but the police had nothing to go on, so he wasn't detained.'

'Was there an inquest?' Theresa asked.

'Yes. It was held in Great Yarmouth. They did it there to avoid the court being turned into a bear pit. There was a lot of local ill feeling about the way the police handled it. There were sirens and policemen all over the place.'

'What was the court's decision?'

'Death by accident. The theory was that she was running down the stairs and banged her head on the beam … but she could just as easily have been pushed down the stairs and caught her head as she was falling. The day before, Carl had been seen arguing with her in the road, which was why the police wanted to question him. His alibi was that he was working; driving his tractor, but he could have left his work for half an hour or so.'

'Did your Michael used to live in the village, then?'

'Yes, but he left years ago. I suppose this is all a coincidence, but Judith bought the cottage from Michael's cousin.'

'I suppose Michael was telling you that Billy was innocent?'

'No, that was the funny thing. He just said that it was possible that he had killed her by accident. Apparently, he has a bit of a temper, but he did love her and just wanted her back.'

Just then, the landlord appeared with the wine list.' Would you like to see the wine list, sir?'

Again, Theresa felt affronted that this man assumed that it was the man's place to order the wine, so before Danny could answer, she said 'We'll have the Pinot Grigio.' She had already looked at the wine list the night before.

The landlord was a bit taken aback by her abruptness and looked at Danny for confirmation, but Danny just nodded in agreement.

'Was that necessary?' Danny asked after he had left.

'Yes. I didn't like his patronising attitude. We're both having fish, so a white wine is best. Anyway, I didn't think you liked seafood?'

'I was persuaded to try the Sea Bass when I was in Norwich and I quite liked it.'

'How many times did you stay overnight in Norwich?'

'Just the once. I told you I avoided staying overnight again.'

'Yes, but you also said you drank red wine – with Sea Bass?'

Danny looked at her for a minute before answering. 'What's this? Why all these questions? Are you trying to catch me out or something? I had a glass of the house white with my main course, while Michael had a glass of red with his steak. And then we moved on to a bottle of red. You know that jealousy is a dreadful thing. It can eat away at you and make you do and say things you wouldn't normally. This isn't like you.'

Theresa reflected on this for a moment. Then said, 'No, I suppose not. The last few weeks have messed with my mind a little.'

'And mine!' Danny responded. Danny was absolutely correct. She had turned into some kind of jealous fiend. She had been checking Danny's mail and his e-mail account. She had also searched her memory bank for any past misdemeanours that would add fuel to her jealous passion, but there had been none – just that one episode of text messages.

The wine appeared. The landlord asked 'Do you want to try it?' This time he addressed his question to both parties.

'No, that's fine,' replied Danny. The landlord filled both glasses and left the bottle.

'What's all this *Tess* business?' Danny asked.

'It's me trying to get into the role of my new main character in my next book.' Then Theresa told him about *Tess of the Dormobiles.*

'That sounds like a good story if you can make it work,' said Danny. 'But it's not an original idea. It's what's known as a Mondegreen.'

'What's one of those?' Theresa asked.

'It's where someone mishears a word or phrase from a

38

song for example. The name Mondegreen comes from a verse which should have read something like *laid him on the green*, I think it was, but someone thought it was *Lady Mondegreen*. So that's what it's been known as ever since – a bit like a malapropism. The one that springs to my mind is the Bob Dylan song – *the ants are my friends.* If you look it up on the internet, I'm sure you'll find dozens more.'

'So if my next book is called *Diamonds are for Heather*, that would be a Mondegreen, would it?'

Danny chuckled. 'Yes, I like that one. But I have heard of *Tess of the Dormobiles* before.'

Theresa felt thoroughly deflated. 'I thought this was a brilliant and original idea.'

Danny could see that Theresa had taken this news badly. 'I don't think anyone has actually tried to turn it into a book. I think it could work ... and I think you're the person to do it.' Danny also had a recollection of *Diamonds are for Heather* being used as a title for an episode of *Only Fools and Horses*, but he kept quiet about that one.

'What about this one?' Theresa asked. 'It's about a young boy who finds an injured seabird; nurses it back to health and finds it to be clever enough to perform tricks. It would be called *Sharp Seagull*.'

Danny looked blank. 'No, I don't get it.'

'I thought you were a fan of the Richard Sharpe novels. You know – like *Sharpe's Rifles*; *Sharpe's Regiment*, and so on.'

Still Danny looked puzzled – and then the penny dropped. 'Oh, you mean *Sharpe's Eagle*. I struggled with that one. I'm not sure people are aware of all the individual Sharpe titles. You might need to re-think that one.'

'Yes, I suppose you're right.'

The food was brought to their table and the conversation slowed and was directed to the quality of the meal.

As they neared the end of their main course, Theresa asked 'So, how are things at work?'

'Depressing! We're steadily getting outnumbered by the Indians, so the camaraderie has gone. Most of the old faces have disappeared for various reasons, so we don't get the office banter like we used to. Don't get me wrong, the Indians are friendly enough, but every now and then, they disappear into a little huddle and start speaking their own language. That makes you think they're saying something they don't want us to hear. Of course, that may not be the case, but you can't help thinking it, so it makes for a very awkward relationship.

To make matters worse, they want to keep all the work to themselves as their way of learning the job, so I'm mostly scraping around for things to do.'

'Is your job under threat, then?' Theresa asked.

'We've been told it isn't. They don't want to make anyone redundant because if the media were to find out, rumours would start about the company being in trouble, which would hit share prices and affect business. They are trying to create new positions for those who want to stay, but not necessarily in IT. I might join a new team that's going to monitor the SLA.'

'What's an SLA?'

'The Service Level Agreement … it stipulates the level of support and performance that VIS has to adhere to, but they keep fiddling statistics to show that they are meeting all their targets. Last week, one of the servers was down and twenty pubs couldn't communicate with head office. It was down for two hours, which is forty hours total across the twenty pubs, but they recorded it as a single incident of just two hours, which is just within their target. That was just one example of what's happening. Of course, the IT Director is telling everybody that the outsourcing is a resounding success and is providing a better service, which everyone knows is a blatant lie, but it makes his decision to outsource look good.

You remember Tom Knowles don't you? He used to work

for another outsourcing company – or 'managed services' as some of them like to call themselves. He said that while there, he overheard one of their Project Managers asking another Project Manager if he could book time to his customer, because his project had gone over budget. In other words, he wanted to charge one customer for time spent on another customer's work. Things like that were happening all the time. He said he was glad to leave them as he felt they were operating immorally.

One of their clients was a government agency. He wouldn't tell me which one because he had to sign a non-disclosure agreement when he went to work for them. This client had been making a right pigs' ear of their development, so the government decided to outsource to his company, but they took on the employees who had been cocking things up, so the same level of incompetence continued. After two years, when the project was still way behind schedule, they lost the contract to another outsourcing company. And guess what? The same employees were transferred to the new company, so things carried on as before. All the time, you and I are paying for these shenanigans through our taxes.'

Just then, the landlord re-appeared and asked if everything was satisfactory. He met with a positive re-action and Theresa asked for the bill.

'Could you ask for redundancy?' Theresa asked Danny after the landlord had disappeared.

'No. They are determined that there will be no redundancies. They don't mind if people leave of their own accord, but definitely no redundancies. One chap persuaded to take early retirement with a full pension even though he was only 59, but he had to sign a document to say he would never tell anyone why he had been asked to leave. But he told me before he signed the document, so he wasn't doing anything wrong by telling me.

So as you can imagine, it's been a miserable few months for me.'

The bill arrived and Theresa had her credit card ready to swipe.

As they walked back to the cottage, Theresa reached for Danny's hand. Danny clenched his other hand into a fist and silently mouthed 'Yes!'

Chapter 6

'Do you want coffee or hot chocolate?' Theresa asked.

'Chocolate, please,' replied Danny, following her into the small kitchen diner area of the cottage. 'I need a good night's sleep. I have to be up early tomorrow. I need to be away by seven at the latest. Have you made up the spare bed?'

'It hasn't been aired properly. You don't need to sleep in the spare bed.'

Danny's eyes lit up and he put his arms around her waist. Then she added 'I thought you'd be better on the settee.'

Danny stopped in his tracks and stared at her.

'I'm kidding,' she said and when he pulled her closer to him, she added 'No, the armchair's probably better.'

This time, he knew she was joking and he kissed her on her forehead.

'I'd better make the drinks,' she said gently pushing him aside.

When she had finished stirring the chocolate, Danny was back with his arms around her. 'Now, where were we?' he said, not expecting an answer. This time, his lips met hers and he held her tightly. Theresa draped her arms around him.

'Here it comes,' she thought to herself and sure enough, his hands wandered down to her buttocks. As a special treat, she clenched her buttocks together.

'Phwooah!' he said. 'I've missed that. They're like two bowling balls!'

'Come on, tiger,' she said. 'Pick up your mug and sit down in the lounge. I think we need to talk about things.'

As they sat down, Danny said 'I'm thinking it's time I went home, don't you?'

Theresa didn't argue, but just said 'I'm staying on here to

43

work on my book, but I need to go home for the weekend. For one thing, I need to get my specs repaired and that means a trip into Stamford on Saturday.'

'We could have lunch at The George,' Danny, said enthusiastically. One would be hard pressed to find somewhere more expensive than the George Hotel in Stamford.

'That's a bit extravagant, isn't it? If you lose your job, we're going to need all the money we have. In any case, I also want to pop into work and see if they've clinched that housing contract … and I need to catch up on my e-mail messages. I've no internet connection here, so I need to spend some time doing all that. We can go out for a meal in the evening if you like … or maybe get a takeaway?'

'I was thinking we could celebrate by going out on the town.'

'Danny! You celebrate! Your idea of a night on the tiles usually involves grouting!'

That was true. Danny had always felt that they were spending so much on their mortgage that it was only right that they enjoyed their cosy little home whenever possible.

'All right,' he said. 'We'll have an Indian takeaway. To be honest, I just want to get back to normal again and put this all behind us.'

'That means you'll be watching *Match of the Day* as usual, then?' she asked.

'I can always record it if you have other ideas,' he said, snuggling up to her. 'Anyway, what was it you wanted us to talk about?'

'I think we've just covered it. I want you to go back home … mainly to look after the cat. I've had to leave Mrs Saunders looking after him, but she's just popping in once a day to feed him. She won't be giving him any fuss. I don't think she likes cats.'

'Is that the main reason you want me back home?'

'No, there are a few other reasons. For one thing the lawn will need mowing. It doesn't stop growing because we're not there.'

Danny knew she was teasing him. 'Are you sure there isn't a leaky tap that needs mending?'

'No, I made sure that was all right before I kicked you out. What time will you be getting up in the morning?'

'About six.'

'There's probably just one slice of toast each, so make sure you leave me one. There are some cereals but go easy on the milk … and I think there's one small glass of juice for each of us. I'm going to get some groceries tomorrow. Make sure I'm up before you leave – just in case I've got some more jobs for you to do at home. Now drink your chocolate and get ready for bed. You've got one more little job tonight if you play your cards right.'

Danny leaned over and kissed her. 'I love you,' he said.

'Yeah, well, I love you,' she replied, dismissively.

When Theresa came down in the morning, Danny was just finishing his toast. 'I'll be coming home Friday evening,' she said.

'How far have you got with this new book?' Danny asked.

'I'm still at the planning stage. To be honest, I still don't have any sort of plot. Perhaps I should have hired a campervan and gone to Dorset.'

'You could base the story in Norfolk. Set it in a fictional village and let your imagination run riot,' Danny suggested.

'Well, I might even do that, but I'm still looking for some inspiration, which is why I want to hang on here for a while longer.'

'I could get a couple of days off next week if you like and we could go off exploring.'

'No, I'm not here for a holiday. I've got to use this time to do some sort of research. I can do the actual writing back home. Some of the local characters have set a seed of an idea, but there's not enough material, yet.'

'Well, you know best,' he said as he got up to leave. 'I'd better get going. I want to get past Lynn before the traffic gets too bad.'

Theresa got ready for a drive over to Hunstanton, but first, she thought she would stroll down to the village shop. The ham she had bought there had been delicious and she always liked to buy local produce whenever possible. As she approached the shop, she noticed that it was called *Throwers*. Where had she heard that name just recently? That was right … Billy's ex-girlfriend was Lynn Thrower. Perhaps the owner was related. She considered it would be too indelicate to mention the death to the storekeeper, but as she entered the shop, she realised that if she wanted to find out what happens in this village, it might provide some useful information. After all, hadn't she been told that Lynn's death had split the village? She needed to hear how the family viewed the situation.

In the shop, there was one other customer who was just paying for her goods. Theresa said 'Good Morning' to both occupants.

'What would you like?' asked the storekeeper, a middle-aged, slim lady wearing glasses.

'I'd like some more of that nice ham, please. About six slices should do fine. Tell me, I noticed the shop is called *Throwers*. Is that any relation to the young lady who met her death in the village?'

'Yes. That was my niece - a lovely young girl.'

'That must have been a horrible shock to you all. I'm so sorry. They say it was an accident, didn't they?'

'You're not another reporter, are you?' the lady enquired, suddenly scowling at Theresa. 'We've had enough of those.'

'No, I'm just staying in the village for a few weeks,' Theresa replied.

'So how do you know about Lynn?'

'Someone was talking about it in the pub the other night. I didn't mean to pry.'

'No, well, I didn't mean to be unfriendly, but it upset a lot of people. We had the police questioning everyone. We're not used to that attention in this village. So, yes, they say it was an accident.'

Theresa detected doubt in the lady's voice. 'But you're not sure, are you?'

'I'm not qualified to judge, but I have some doubts.'

'Why is that?'

'She is said to have banged her head on the beam near the top of the stairs … and, yes, her blood was found on the beam, but she'd lived in that house for over twenty years. Why should she suddenly hit her head that day? It doesn't make sense.'

'Could she have been running downstairs to answer the door or the telephone?'

'They checked the telephone records, so it wasn't that. The thing was … she was seen in the street the day before, having a heated argument with Billy. He's got a heck of a temper on him. Most of the time, you think he's a normal quiet lad; not the brightest person you'll ever meet, but he wouldn't normally say *boo* to a goose. However, I've seen him when he's lost it and he could be quiet frightening. I had to throw him out of here one day.'

'Why was that?' Theresa asked.

'Well, Lynn had already split up with him because of his jealousy. This was because, one night in the pub … he was always in the pub … used to drink a lot before he lost his job. Now he can only afford a half a pint a night, but he still goes down the pub most nights. Anyway, this one night, some of the lads were talking about wanting something or other for their car, I think it was and one lad said '*You can get what you want from Lynn*' – meaning, of course, King's Lynn, but Billy

47

already worse for wear, took it the wrong way and started a fight.

That was the last straw for Lynn and she broke off their engagement. She'd already had a few disagreements due to his unwarranted jealousy. A few days later, he was in this shop and some of the lads saw an opportunity to wind him up. One of them said *'I went up Lynn last Saturday … had a great night.'*

I think Billy probably knew it was a wind-up, but he still wanted to punch someone's lights out. So I told him to get outside and not come back until he'd learnt to control himself. He hasn't been back in here, since.'

'I noticed him staring at me the other night. I must admit it looked a little scary.'

'Oh, that's because he won't wear his glasses. He wasn't staring at you. He was just staring towards you. He can't see a thing without glasses.'

'Why doesn't he wear his glasses?'

'Vanity! He wants to be a lady's man like his brother. The thing is that even without his glasses, he's still not very good looking. Michael's the one with the looks in that family.'

'So Michael's a lady's man?' Theresa asked. This didn't sound right for someone who had propositioned her husband.

'He thinks he is. Personally, I find him a bit smarmy.'

'But he's married with a family, isn't he?'

'Yes, do you know him?'

'No, I don't personally, but he works with my husband.'

'Well, he may be married, but he'll chase anything that moves – male; female; probably animal, if you ask me. He's not normal – a real *Tommy Twoways.*'

'You wouldn't know which way to turn with someone like that,' Theresa joked, hoping this lady wouldn't be offended by such smutty humour, but the shopkeeper chuckled and entered the price of the ham in the till. By now, an elderly gentleman had entered the shop and was waiting to be served.

'Sorry, was there anything else?'

'No, that's it for today. I'll let you serve this gentleman. I'll see you soon.'

As Theresa strolled back to the cottage, she pondered what she'd just heard. So the malevolency of Billy's stare had been in her imagination, but, with his terrible temper, that didn't rule out the possibility of him being responsible for Lynn's death. And he did follow Theresa home that night. That was certainly scary.

Just before she reached the cottage, she could see Mrs Fitheridge approaching. She was the lady who looked after the cottage in between bookings. She was a fussy looking little woman of about fifty to fifty-five years of age. 'Hello Theresa,' she said. 'Have you just been to the shop? I'm just going myself. They're not the cheapest place around, but it's very handy and their goods are always of the highest quality. I'm going to get some of their orgasmic bread. It's made with wheat that's never seen any pestilences of any kind.'

Theresa had noticed that Mrs Fitheridge usually spoke so quickly that she didn't always use the correct words. It took Theresa a second to realise that she had meant *organic* and *pesticides*. Theresa didn't normally bother to correct her, but on this occasion, she said 'Well, if they've got some orgasmic bread, I think I'll go back and get some.'

'Did I say *orgasmic*? Oh dear. Whatever must you think of me? I think if they sold orgasmic bread, they'd soon run out. Are you going sightseeing, today?'

'I'm going over to Hunstanton to get some groceries, so I might have a wander round there, but I'm not on holiday, so I mustn't enjoy myself too much.'

'I should make the most of it while you can. It's going to rain, tomorrow. I can tell by the cloud formulations. I've lived here long enough to recognise the weather patterns. You see if I'm not wrong.'

'In that case, 'Theresa said, 'I'd better get on with my day. It's nice to see you again,' and she carried on before Mrs Fitheridge could start up again.

Despite telling Danny she wasn't in Norfolk for a holiday, she couldn't resist extending her trip to Hunstanton to include a wander around and after buying sufficient groceries to see her through the next few days, she parked near the green. Her first indulgence was to buy herself fish and chips. As she sat on a bench in the middle of the green, she wondered why fish and chips tasted so much better when eaten at the seaside.

Hunstanton was already starting to wind down for the winter. Her grandfather had often talked about his excursions when he was younger; when the pier was still intact and the huge outdoor swimming pool was a major attraction. He had told her that the pool had contained salt-water, which added to the appeal. He and his mates would catch a train from Peterborough, changing at Lynn and arriving within a few hundred yards of the promenade where the pool had once existed. The trains were always busy in the summer months, so it was a mystery to him why the line was closed in the sixties.

Theresa tried to imagine what the pier would have looked like in its heyday. Apparently, a small train ran along its length, but this was removed in the fifties. Later, the pier was damaged; firstly by storm, leaving a short remnant and then later by fire. The building that sits on the site now is still referred to as the pier, but that is totally misleading.

Theresa was very tempted to drive further around the coast to visit one or two of the lovely little villages, but she had told Danny that this was not a holiday and she still hadn't made much progress on her book.

As she drove back to Bircham St. Mary, she made up her mind that if the occasion arose, she would attempt to talk to Billy. What she had heard about him intrigued her – almost bothered her, but if she wanted to find a villain for her novel, perhaps he might inspire her. However, she promised herself that she would only talk to him in public. She wouldn't allow him to frighten her on a dark road again. Now that she was re-united with Danny, she felt a renewed confidence ... and she was happy again.

Chapter 7

'Could I have a half of cider, please?' Theresa asked of the landlord, after she had exchanged greetings with Eddie and Millie who no longer occupied their usual place at the bar since this had been taken by a young couple who were busy reading a menu. Eddie and Millie were seated just opposite Billy who was alone in his usual corner position. He was quietly supping his half of beer and staring in his customary manner, which Theresa still found a little creepy.

'Can I join you?' Theresa asked of Eddie and Millie.

'Only if you agree to give up your place if Angelina Jolie wants to sit there,' Eddie joked.

'Does she come here a lot?' Theresa asked.

'She used to,' replied Millie, 'but she got fed up with Eddie's jokes.

'Where's the old man?' Eddie asked.

'He's gone back home. It was only a quick visit,' Theresa replied.

'Have you been busy writing today?' asked Millie.

'Not really. I had to pop over to Hunstanton for a few things.'

'I remember being on Hunstanton beach once,' said Eddie. 'There were all these young women wearing bikinis and I remarked to Millie that there weren't much difference between wearing a bikini and wearing bra and panties. So I didn't see any reason why someone shouldn't wear bra and knickers on a beach. She said *'Yes, there is … so take them off. You look ridiculous.'*

Everyone laughed. And even Billy had a smile on his face.

'Did you go in the fairground?' Millie enquired.

'No, I just did a bit of shopping … and then had some fish and chips.'

'Several years ago,' Millie continued, 'we took our nephew on the Ghost Train. You know what these things are like … all dark and funny noises. Wayne wasn't very impressed. And then this woman appeared out of the dark and started following our little car and ruffling Wayne's hair. He just turned round to her and said *"Pack it in. You're not scary. You're just annoying!"* He was only about nine years old.'

'I suspect she got a lot of people reacting like that,' said Theresa. 'It can't have been much fun for her.'

'This new book of yours …' Eddie suddenly interrupted as he was inclined to do,' what's it about?'

'I can't really say at the moment.' Theresa didn't want to appear secretive, but she didn't want to reveal the title at this stage and she still didn't have any plot worth talking about.

'Is it set around here?' Eddie asked.

'I don't know just yet. Is this a good place for interesting stories? Any good local ghost stories or smuggling … anything like that?'

'You know *Cherry Tree Cottage* is haunted, don't you?' Eddie replied.

'He's just joking,' Millie said, when she saw the look on Theresa's face, but Theresa noticed Billy had suddenly looked up from his drink. 'Anyway,' continued Millie, 'to answer your question, it's always been very quiet around here, but there was that vicar fellow from Stiffkey.'

'Stukey!' correct Eddie. 'It's pronounced *Stukey.'*

'I say *Stiffkey,'* reiterated Millie.

'The correct pronounciation is *Stukey*!' Eddie said insistently.

'You can't even pronounce *pronunciation!'* Millie said, as they all laughed at him.

'Well, we'll ask Les,' said Eddie. 'Les!' he shouted at the landlord, who was busy speaking to the couple with the menu.

'Just a minute, Eddie,' Les replied with more patience than Theresa thought was deserved.

After a few minutes, Les finished talking to the couple and said 'Yes Eddie. What is it?'

'Is it *Stukey* or *Stiffkey*?' Eddie asked.

'Either,' replied Les.

'No … one of them must be correct. What do all the locals use?'

'I've heard both being used by locals. I personally think that those who say *Stukey* just can't be bothered to say it properly.'

'A bit like *Hunst'n* instead of *Hunstanton*,' chipped in Theresa, who remembered being confused when she had first heard people talking about *Hunst'n* which wasn't on any map she could find.

'Yes,' replied Les. 'That's about it. But then some say Norwich is *Narridge*. It's just a dialect sort of thing.

'So we were both right, then,' said Millie.

'No, my way is correct,' said Eddie.

'Yeah, but then you would argue with a signpost,' Millie added.

'Anyway,' said Theresa, 'What about this vicar?'

'Well, he decided to care for fallen women,' said Millie. 'But, his involvement with them was said to be a bit more than just *caring* if you follow me.'

'I don't remember reading about this,' said Theresa.

'Well, you wouldn't. This was soon after the first world war.'

'Is that the only interesting story around here - something that happened nearly a century ago?'

'Well, it's always a bit quiet around here.' Millie wanted to mention Lynn Thrower's death, but she could tell that Billy was listening to every word they said. 'If you want more information about this vicar, I'm sure you can find it on the internet. Just search for *vicar at Stiffkey.*'

'Stukey!' chipped in Eddie.

'If you search on *Stukey,* you won't find anything. It's spelt S-T-I-F-F-K-E-Y.'

Theresa noticed that Eddie was quickly downing his beer, so she asked 'Can I get you two a drink?'

'No, it's very kind of you, dear,' Millie replied, 'but we have to be off. We've got an early start tomorrow. We're going up to Yorkshire for a few days to see Eddie's family.'

Eddie struggled to stand up and reached for his stick. 'I think you'd better fetch the car. I don't think my knees can manage it.'

'Come on! You know the doctor said you've got to get more exercise. It's not that far. You know,' she said to Theresa, 'he thinks that lifting a glass of beer counts as weight training. That's why he always drinks pints – because their heavier!'

'I'll have you know that I'm the proud possessor of a six-pack,' Eddie announced.

'That's not a six-pack,' Millie said. 'It's a Lurpak! Look at the belly on that!'

'My doctor says I've got a large intestine,' Eddie responded.

'We've all got a large intestine, you silly old bugger, you.'

Theresa had the impression that these jokes had been told many times, but she still laughed.

'Have a good break,' she said as she opened the door for Eddie to hobble through.

She and Billy were now the only two people still in the bar, and feeling this might be awkward, Theresa decided she would try to talk to him. She was quite anxious about this, but she steeled herself to go through with it.

'It's a bit quiet in here, tonight,' she said.

Billy looked around to make sure that Theresa was, in fact, talking to him. His reply demonstrated his embarrassment at being spoken to out of the blue like that. 'Aah … it's usually quiet mid-week... usually more here at the weekend.' Theresa still found his high-pitched voice a little strange. Billy gulped the last remains of his beer and shuffled as though it was time to go.

Theresa pre-empted this and gulped her own last mouthful and asked 'Can I get you another?'

'Aah … well, no – see, I can't afford to buy you one, so if I can't pays me way, I prefer to just buy me own drinks.'

'I'm not expecting you to buy me one. I just want to chat to you about my book. What are you drinking?'

'I.P.A.,' was the hesitant reply.

Theresa bought him a pint of beer. Billy looked even more embarrassed when he saw a full pint in front of him and as Theresa sat next to him, Billy, relieved of the purgatory of making half pints last all evening, took a giant gulp and half a pint had disappeared in an instant. 'Aah … 'at's nice!' he gasped. 'Thank you.' Then he went back to sipping the remainder of his beer at his more accustomed pace. 'I'm out of work, see,' he added. 'I don't get much money on the jobseekers allowance, so I can't stand a round of drinks. They're trying to stop me money because I can't get any work 'round here and I can't drive; so …' he shrugged despondently.

'What skills have you got?' Theresa asked.

'Just farm work. 'Ats all I've ever done. I got some good grades on me GCSEs, but they see farm work on my CV, and tha's the only thing they think I c'n do.'

'Can't you re-train? What about that CITB place down the road at Bircham Newton? Couldn't you learn to be a brickie – or even a brickie's labourer? I hear they're hard to find these days. I think you have to apply for grants. You might get an apprenticeship.'

'I don't know,' he replied.

'Why don't you look it up on the internet?'

'Haven't got a compooter. I suppose I could ask my brother to look into it.'

'Is Michael your elder brother?' Theresa wanted to change the subject because Billy's whole attitude about work seemed so negative.

'Yeah, he's five years older.' There was a bit of a pause before he added 'He's not me real brother.'

'Really?'

'No. At least we don't have the same father. I found his birth certif'cate while I was looking for mine one day. It were with me parents' marriage certif'cate. They got wed just afore I were born. Michael's was five years earlier. His father's name was Coviello. I think that's Italian – probably explains why he's one for the ladies.'

'I thought he was married with children?' Theresa, of course, already knew of his proclivity for philandering, but she wanted to know more.

'He is. Don't stop him though! He can't help himself. He says it's an illness. I wish I had his luck with girls. He's better than me at everything – better looking; more intelligent – he went to University; got a good job and a lovely wife and children. Mind you, I've always been able to better him in a scrap. I first beat him when I was twelve and he were seventeen. He hasn't dared tackle me since our teens.'

'Do you fight very often?'

'No, we get on ever so well. He's always looked after me. No, I don't like fighting. I don't like hurting anything.' This seemed to confirm that, indeed, Billy was *harmless*, except that Lynn's aunt did say he had a temper, especially when he was jealous.

'So did you enjoy reading my novel?' Theresa asked, thinking it was time to change the subject.

'Your novel? Yeah, I did.'

'What did you like about it?'

Billy thought about this for a few moments. 'It had a happy ending.'

'Anything else?'

'Um … I can't think of anything else.'

'Well, what made you read it?'

'Michael said I should read it.'

'Why did he think that?'

'He said it might cheer me up. It was about a chap who was feeling sorry for himself because he didn't have a girlfriend. Michael thought I might – what was the word - *empathise*.' Billy seemed pleased with himself for remembering the word.

'And did you?'

'I don't know. I'm not sure what *empathise* means.'

'I suppose it means share someone's feelings. So did you?'

'Yeah, I suppose so. I lost my girlfriend last year and I've been very miserable since.'

'Did you love her very much?'

'Err … yeah, I think so. She was lovely. The nicest person you could ever meet. Everyone said so. She didn't have a bad word to say about anyone. Trouble is … I think people took advantage of her. All the other lads in the village tried to get off with her.'

Theresa wanted to explore this aspect of their relationship, so she asked 'Did that make you jealous?'

'Yeah, I suppose so. It weren't that I didn't trust Lynn. I did, but I'm not sure I trusted the other blokes to try it on, you know. She just wanted to be friends with everyone. Lynn and me had been together for ages – since we went to school and as Mr Thrower – Lynn's father – didn't have any other children, he encouraged me to leave school as soon as possible to work on his farm. She was going to inherit the farm when he died, so he wanted to know it would be in good hands. When she died, tha' all changed. He said I weren't doing very well and I didn't have a licence to take the tractor on the road. It were true that my heart weren't in it like before, but I think he had other plans for the farm. He's got one of Lynn's cousins doing my work, now. If I'd known what would happen, I'd have stayed on at school and got better qualifications.'

Billy had been nervously sipping his beer and by now, he

was down to the last mouthful which he finished off. 'Thanks for the drink,' he said. 'And …' he paused.

'Yes?'

'Thanks for talking to me. Not many people round here bother with me.'

'That's all right. I've enjoyed it. Do you know, the first time I saw you, you frightened me?'

Billy looked surprised. 'Me? What did I do?'

'Well, for a start, you kept staring at me. Then you followed me home and then I saw you staring up at my cottage.'

'I'm … sorry.' Theresa decided that Billy seemed to be one of those men who struggled to apologise, so he must have meant it. 'I should wear glasses, see, so I didn't realise I was staring. I was following you 'cause I was plucking up the nerve to talk to you about your book. I've never met an author before.' Theresa wondered about this because he hadn't actually said much about the book.

'And,' he continued, 'I were looking at the cottage because it were me aunt's house and I used to spend a lot of time 'round there. I wondered what it looked like since it were done up. I didn't realise I were scaring you. Honest!'

'Well, maybe I let my imagination run away with me. Anyway, I'd better be on my way, now.'

'I'm just leaving,' Billy said as he finished his last gulp of beer. 'Can I walk with you? I'll make sure no one else scares you.'

'Yes, all right.' Theresa wanted to say 'no', but she couldn't see how without causing offence. Had it been any previous evening of that week, she would definitely have declined the suggestion, but now she could see that her fears had all been misplaced.

As they walked along, Theresa asked 'Do you do much reading?'

'I do a lot more these days – now that I'm out o' work.

There's a mobile library comes round the village.'

'What sort of thing do you normally read?'

'Varies. Whatever I like the look of. Historical fiction is probably me favourite.'

'So that's what you do all day, is it?'

'That and a bit of telly. I like the daytime quizzes.' Theresa realised that her early impression of Billy as an ignorant country bumpkin was not entirely accurate.

'My grandfather liked to watch those,' she said. 'He got annoyed if the contestants weren't very bright and he hoped they would lose. And if they were very clever, he hoped they would lose as well, because he didn't like know-alls. He did always support the pretty young girls, though. He was the chap who inspired my book.'

'Did he have a happy ending?' Billy asked.

'Is there really such a thing? He survived my grandmother by nearly ten years and he missed her every single day of that time. He did find a good companion, but she was only a friend and couldn't hope to replace his wife.'

'I suppose I will still be missing Lynn in ten years' time,' Billy said wistfully.

Theresa realised that she had touched a raw nerve. 'No, I'm sure you'll have found someone else well before then,' she said.

There was now a lull in the conversation as they neared the cottage and for some reason, Theresa desperately wanted to avoid a silence, so she asked 'Why don't you wear your glasses?'

'Lynn said she preferred me without them … and now I s'pose I keep forgetting to wear them. P'raps I should if I'm scaring folk!' He said this last sentence with a chuckle. Then he added 'You know Eddie's talk of *Cherry Tree Cottage* being haunted is a load of old squit, don't you?'

'Yes, he was just trying to be amusing.'

'When we were young, me and Michael would spend each

Sunday afternoon with me aunt and uncle. We were glad to get out of the house when me dad came home from the pub Sunday lunchtime. Aunt Lesley kept loads of games for us to play with and she always had a new card game to show us. She had a box of pre-decimal pennies that she would share out so that we could gamble.'

'I had an aunt like that. The rest of the family made fun of her, but she was great with all the youngsters.' By now they were right outside the cottage. 'Sometime, you'll have to come inside and see what it looks like with the extension – but not tonight, if you don't mind.'

'I'd like that. Thanks again for talking to me.'

'That's quite all right. Goodnight.'

Once inside, Theresa wanted to make a note of some of Eddie's little quips, so she found a piece of paper and wrote 'Bra & panties,' 'Lurpak' and 'large intestine.' She thought she might include these in her book, which she now decided was going to be a comedy thriller adventure story, even though she was no further with finding a plot for it.

Chapter 8

As Theresa entered the *Bittern*, she was met with the sight of Danny sitting in a compromising position with Eddie who was wearing nothing but a bra and panties and looking in very good condition for his age. Meanwhile, Millie was sitting in the corner, being willingly seduced by Michael. None of them seemed to be aware of Theresa entering and even when the landlord greeted her with his usual 'Hello Tess,' nobody else seemed to care about her presence.

She was so upset at the sight of all this that she ran from the pub out into the road, which was now back in her home village of Woodnewton. Her feet felt leaden and although she was trying desperately to run as fast as she could, her progress was painfully slow. Every footfall seemed to sink into the pavement as though it were made of quicksand. She was now aware that Billy had followed her out of the pub and was rapidly gaining on her. She didn't dare look round, but she knew he had a machete in his hand. To make matters worse, she desperately needed to use the toilet.

A public toilet suddenly appeared. This must have been recently erected because no public convenience had ever existed in this village, but her relief was turned to dismay when she discovered a pay barrier prevented her entry and she had no money. Billy was behind her brandishing a twenty pence coin, but he wanted something in return, so she pushed past him and headed towards her own house, which wasn't where she had left it.

Suddenly, she was aware of a tractor going past *Cherry Tree Cottage* and so she awoke to reality, needing to use the toilet.

She decided she shouldn't have had that second glass of cider the previous evening and after relieving herself, she sat down on the bed to clear her thoughts. Theresa was not given to believe in the magic meaning of dreams, but they must have indicated some sort of subconscious thoughts. She thought she had accepted Danny's explanation for his liaison with Michael, yet here she was dreaming of him in a compromising position with another man. Was this just silly jealousy eating at her still? And there was Billy still showing signs of menace, despite their cosy little chat of the previous evening. How did she recognise Michael in her dream when she's never met him? The mind was a mysterious organ.

The one thing that was not a surprise was the impossible tiredness in her limbs when she was being chased. This was a frequent occurrence in her dreams and harked back to the time when she had contracted glandular fever; a disease that had returned many times during the months after the doctor had told her that her blood tests had revealed no further trace of the illness. She could be walking along feeling perfectly all right, then she would gradually be overcome with such fatigue that she needed to stop and rest before she could continue. After a year, the symptoms disappeared, but the memory of that sensation still haunted her.

As she ate her breakfast, she contemplated her plans for the day. With Millie and Eddie going away for a few days, she would avoid the *Bittern*. She didn't want to visit a half-empty pub and find herself talking to Billy again. That would look all wrong. Although she had told Danny she wasn't there on holiday, she still fancied exploring the region a bit more. For one thing, if she was to base her story in Norfolk, she wanted to find some places where her fictitious Tess could park her campervan. If she couldn't find any actual places, she would use her imagination to invent a village location.

Then she had a thought. She remembered an incident several years earlier when she and Danny had visited Blakeney. It was a lovely summer evening and they had parked their car on the Quayside car park while they went for a relaxing stroll along the raised bank beside the creek, admiring the many yachts and dinghies and listening to the soft, but persistent clanging of the rigging in the gentle evening breeze. A passer-by enthusiastically told them that he had just seen a marsh harrier threatening the skies, but they were not fortunate enough to witness the same sight.

When they returned to their vehicle, they found that several cars were standing in water. The exceptional tide had caught a few visitors unaware and they would need towing out. Fortunately, Danny had parked slightly higher up and had escaped this embarrassment, but it was a warning for any future visits.

Theresa decided that in her novel, she could have Tess' campervan trapped by the tide and she would be rescued by some handsome hunky local. In return, she would insist on buying this Adonis a drink in the nearby hostelry. But he had a murky past – something to do with a missing legacy, perhaps? Tess would inadvertently get mixed up in all this. Theresa could develop the plot from there. At least she now had a plot to develop.

However, she wasn't sure if a campervan could be left overnight in that car park, so perhaps a visit to see the parking restrictions could help her answer the question. That was her plan for the day – a drive over to Blakeney to view the parking facilities. She told herself that this was a genuine reason to visit one of her favourite locations.

But then she put her plans on hold, because the sky suddenly darkened; a banshee wind screamed through the old sash windows, and inevitably, a deluge hit Bircham St. Mary's. Mrs Fitheridge's prediction had come true. There is only one thing worse than the seaside in the rain, she decided – and that was the seaside in the rain, out of season. And it was near enough to being out of season to persuade her to rethink her plans for the day. She told herself that she really should start putting some words down on paper – well, on disk, anyway.

Actually, she was feeling quite enthusiastic about developing the character of this hunky Samaritan. She would create him in the image of a man she herself would find totally irresistible. He would be over six feet tall with wide shoulders and a V-shaped back. He would obviously be good looking, but not in a 'pretty-boy' way. She thought of giving him some mysterious gypsy features, such as a swarthy complexion and earrings, but decided that this was too clichéd. No, he would look and sound well educated. Above all, he would have a wicked sense of humour – then Theresa could include some of the jokes she heard in the *Bittern*. Danny, she was sure, would also be a great source of witticisms.

She thought of Danny. She was so pleased that they were back together, but somehow, things would never be the same and it bothered her. Perhaps the fault was all hers, with her silly jealousy. She'd heard of marriages being ruined by jealousy and she knew she had to overcome it. The coming weekend would repair the harm done and she was looking forward to going home and getting back to normal.

For the rest of the day, Theresa never left the cottage and she was able to employ her creativity for the first time that long week. She decided to skip the first few chapters as she still needed to introduce Tess to her campervan and she felt she could use the internet to research that mode of transport, but that would have to wait until the weekend when she would have wi-fi access to the world at large. Starting part way through a novel wasn't the way that Theresa preferred to write. She would have rather had started at the beginning of her story and let the plot and the characters develop, but needs must.

By the end of the day, she had completed a chapter and a half and had set the seeds for a passionate romance between Tess and Toby, whose full name was Tobias Thackeray. Theresa liked the sound of Toby and Tess as a couple – a bit like Porgy and Bess and she started singing 'I loves you Toby' in a deep voice trying to sound like Nina Simone.

Toby had been raised in a middle-class environment and had set up in business as a management consultant, until after several years, disillusionment brought a change of life style. He had started out on his career full of enthusiasm to improve management throughout the U.K., but he soon discovered that employers disapproved of an outsider coming in and criticising their management techniques. Instead, what they mostly looked for was an outsider to back up their unpopular policies and take the blame for their actions. Toby therefore had a choice – to lose business by doing the job his way or making a good living by being someone's scapegoat. He decided to opt out of the rat race and chose a more frugal lifestyle, living on his wits in Norfolk. He bought a small dinghy, which he hired out for fishing trips for the casual tourist and lived in an old caravan, which resided in a friend's field. Toby would help Tess park overnight in the same field. Theresa wasn't sure how realistic this all was, but, in her experience, novels were often unrealistic.

As a result of his 'dropping out', Toby had alienated his parents who had struggled to put him through university, but he was happier than he had ever been. Everyone in the village knew Toby. The village in question was likely to be Burnham St Mary – a fictitious location, loosely based on a combination of Burnham Overy Staithe, Blakeney and Bircham St Mary's, although Theresa thought she might still change her mind and return to her original plan of placing the novel in Dorset. Burnham St Mary sounded like a name that could just as easily come from the West Country.

The pub in the village of Burnham St Mary was the *Fisherman's Arms* and Tess would encounter some of its clientele which would include a loud mouthed Northerner who liked to laugh at his own jokes and had a habit of interrupting people, much to the annoyance of his long-suffering wife. Every night at the *Fisherman's*, a scary looking bloke would sit up a corner on his own. Unlike the real-life Billy, Terry really was malevolent. He and Toby had already crossed swords and now he held a major grudge against Toby, who felt obliged to watch his back at every turn. Theresa still had to think of the history between these two rivals, but that could come in a later chapter when Tess' relationship with Toby had developed enough for him to take her into his confidence.

Theresa had never actually met someone whom she would describe as evil and wondered if such people really did exist. There were lots of people she disliked for various reasons, but none of them could actually be described as evil, so she would have to use her imagination with this.

When evening came, Theresa found she didn't want to stay in the cottage on her own, but she had already decided not to visit the *Bittern*, Instead, she took a quiet stroll in the opposite direction and stopped a few hundred yards outside of the village where the ancient church stood. Like a lot of churches in Norfolk, this one had a delightful little round tower. She had discovered the reason for the proliferation of round towers was the local flint that was used in the construction. To construct a square tower, the builders would have required good quality stone which could be dressed, thus allowing straight corners. This was not possible with flint, but round towers were perfectly feasible.

She wondered why the church was outside the village. By now, the rain had long gone, but the roads and paths were still wet and it was already turning dark. As she turned back towards *Cherry Tree Cottage*, it occurred to her that she would have walked past Billy's house, but she had no idea which one it was.

When she neared the edge of the village, she heard a door opening and hoped it wasn't Billy on his way to the pub. She didn't want to have to make excuses for not visiting the *Bittern* that evening, but it was another gentleman taking his dog for a walk. In fact, it was the same man she had spoken to at the start of the week when Billy was frightening her. He wished her a good evening as he came out of his gate.

Theresa returned the greeting. Then asked 'Do you know why the church is outside the village?'

The man had quite a refined voice. 'There used to be a manor with extensive grounds and the church would have been built for the convenience of the Lord of the Manor rather than the villagers,' he replied.

'What happened to the manor?' Theresa asked.

'Well that was before my time, but I believe it was pulled down when a new owner faced punitive death duties. The land was sold off to the Thrower family to extend their arable land.'

'So the Throwers are the big land owners around here, then?'

'They own all the farming land around here. Get down Scott!' He was shouting at the Scottie who was jumping up Theresa's trousers. 'Don't pat him. It only encourages him to jump at people.'

'So if someone lost their job on their farm, he or she would be unable to find similar work around here?'

'You mean someone like your friend Billy? Yes, he'd have to travel some distance to do the same sort of work. If you're interested in our church, you might make an attempt to find our Green Man. You know what the Green man is, don't you?'

'Isn't that a pagan thing? What's it doing in a Christian church?'

'Lots of churches have them. It may be some kind of hangover from Roman deities. After all, Christmas day is celebrated on the same day as a Roman festival. The Green Man is usually depicted as a head carved into a column or bench or whatever, with a tree or foliage growing out of his face. I'll give you a clue if you do want to look for it. You have to look upwards to find it.'

'I might have a look,' Theresa responded. 'Is the church usually open?'

'It's not open during the week. There's a service every Sunday morning. It's not as well attended as it used to be of course, but that's the same everywhere. Feel free to join us, if you wish.'

'Thank you, Theresa replied, 'but I won't be around this weekend. Do you go every Sunday?'

'Well, I don't go every week, religiously …'

Theresa gave a short laugh and the man stopped speaking, as though offended.

'I'm sorry, she said, 'but you said you don't go *religiously*.'

'Oh yes, so I did … very funny.'

'Well, I'm at my cottage now. Thank you for the information. Good night.'

'Good night, my dear.'

The story of the church in the middle of nowhere and the Green Man gave Theresa some further ideas for her novel to which she returned as soon as she had eaten her breakfast the next day. She wanted to get home to Woodnewton as soon as possible and was tempted to set out quite early, but she considered that it was important to keep writing while the mood was right. When she was writing the first book, she had a couple of spells when she stopped for a while – and it became all too easy to not bother to start again, so this time she would discipline herself to spend at least two hours a day on her new one, even if that was just research.

She finished off the second chapter by late morning; then set off for home, allowing for a lunchtime stop at a superstore on the outskirts of King's Lynn, where she also picked up some groceries. That evening, she intended to cook a special meal for Danny. It was her way of making up for the distress of their unnecessary separation, which she now decided was entirely her fault.

While she was eating, she received a text message asking her to call the office. The message had been sent three days earlier, but had only just arrived when she got back in signal range. As Theresa only had a pay-as-you-go phone, she decided she would call back on her landline when she got home. After all, she was on holiday, but she would call the minute she reached home.

However, when she entered their cottage, she was appalled at the state in which Danny had left the kitchen. Dirty crockery was piled up in the sink and the room smelt of last night's curry, which still splattered the sides of the microwave. After she had cleared everything away, she was in no mood to cook him something special, so she decided they would both have to put up with an omelette.

By the time Danny arrived home, Theresa was even more annoyed and as he draped his arms around her, expecting the same warm, forgiving person he had left on Wednesday morning, he found a cold unforgiving, glaring harridan.

'What's up?' he asked.

'What's up he asks! I leave my home alone for a few days and come back to find it's been turned into a slum! There must have been three days washing up left festering in my sink! My kitchen reeks of curry; the microwave looks like a bilious attack; the cat's dish is filthy and he wouldn't eat out of it until I had scraped all the stale food off it! And you ask what's up!'

'It was one day's washing up, that's all,' Danny replied. 'I was going to do it last night, but I fell asleep in front of the television. I was catching up on some of the sleep I've lost over the last few months, missing you and tearing my guts out. When I woke up, it was after midnight, so I told myself I would do it before I went to work this morning, but then I overslept this morning. I left work with good intentions to tackle it before you came home, but you beat me to it. I'm sorry. Let me take you out for a meal to make up for it.'

But Theresa wasn't going to be bribed out of her indignity. 'You're too late. I'm preparing an omelette. In any case, I haven't time to go out. I have to do some work on the internet and catch up on my e-mails. Damn! I was meant to call the office when I got home, but I've been too busy tidying up your mess. It's too late to call them now. It's all your damned fault. Go and get changed while I finish off this bloody omelette.'

'I really am sorry. Can I just have a kiss?'

'No, you bloody can't!'

But once Danny had changed and returned to the kitchen, Theresa had calmed down.

'This is a lovely omelette,' Danny said.

'It's just an omelette,' she replied, but without the rancour of their previous conversation.

'How's the writing going?' Danny asked.

'It's better now. I've finished two chapters and I know a bit more about where it's heading. Did I tell you it's going to be a comedy-thriller?'

'No. You mentioned the title, but you didn't tell me much more than that.'

'Yes, well, I don't want to make it the run-of-the-mill thriller or whodunit. I want it be something a little different – in keeping with the title, I suppose. So I've been trying to note down a few jokes and funny remarks to include – so I thought you might be able to help me with that.'

'Well, of course I know loads of jokes,' Danny said, 'but I need to know the situations in the book where you want them.'

'I'll try to work out some clues for you,' Theresa replied.

'There is this character in a pub who keeps telling jokes – a bit like that chap Eddie at the *Bittern* – and he just tells jokes all the time, but I don't want any lengthy jokes; just a few one-liners, if possible.'

'I'm sure I can help. Unfortunately, I don't hear so many at work these days. The Indians laugh if you tell them a joke, but they never tell them. Perhaps it's their work ethic.'

'Maybe you should socialise with them?'

'No. They're the enemy. They're taking our jobs away from us. It's one thing being nice to them at work, but none of us want to see them in our own time.'

'Doesn't that sound a bit racist?' Theresa asked.

'No! It doesn't matter where they come from. They're still taking our jobs away from us. It's got nothing to do with race.'

As they finished their omelettes, Danny said 'I'll make a cup of tea and do the washing up. You can get on with the things you wanted to do on the computer.'

'Thank you,' she replied.

Chapter 9

The first thing Theresa was anxious to do that evening was to check her e-mail. If she was away from her computer for any length of time, she would always eagerly anticipate all sorts of interesting correspondence from friends or colleagues telling her how much they had enjoyed reading her book; or her publisher telling her that a wonderful review of her novel had appeared in the national press. But, of course, none of these things ever actually happened – and tonight was no exception. There were several messages from Facebook informing her that Dottie had changed her cover photo; Eric (she couldn't remember whose friend of a friend he was) had a birthday coming up and Marge was at the London Hilton drinking Pimms, none of which was of the slightest interest to Theresa. There was other spam such as a health company telling her she could get a year's supply of multivitamins free with her next order over thirty pounds (she would try once more to unsubscribe - how she regretted ordering those cod liver oil capsules!).

But there was one relevant message from her manager informing her of the good news that the company had secured the Hampton housing contract, so the next few months were going to be very busy for all concerned and could she please cut her holiday short. So that was why she had a text message to contact the office. She thought about this for a few minutes and realised that if she went straight back to work, there was every chance that due to pressure of work, she would not be able to book any more holidays before Christmas, so she decided that she would stay at Bircham for one more week. In any case, she had left some things at *Cherry Tree Cottage* so she had to go back to fetch those. One more week would give her the chance to do some more writing and see a little more of Norfolk. She had to go into Stamford the next day, so she would call in at the office to find out more about the work and tell them of her intentions. For now, she sent a reply, saying 'Message received, I'll be in touch to discuss my holiday plans' and didn't say any more than that.

When Danny brought her cup of tea, Theresa told him the news about the housing contract.

'That's great news,' he said.

'Why do you say that?' she asked.

Danny looked puzzled at her question. 'Well, for a start, it will be good for job security. It will present a chance for some valuable experience … and, from my point of view, you'll have to be at home more, instead of gallivanting across to Norfolk.'

'You think that's what I'm doing – gallivanting?'

'Probably not the right word … I just meant I will see more of you.' Danny realised that Theresa was still a little prickly, so he added 'I'll let you get on with your work. Would you like me to put on some background music?'

'Yes … something relaxing. How about some Earl Klugh? I don't want anything too loud. I want to do some research on campervans.'

Theresa typed '*dormobile*' into her search engine and started her research. She found that the original Dormobile was effectively a converted Bedford van and the company that performed this conversion went on to perform a similar feat with other makes, usually adding an expanding roof, as well as useful accessories such as bunk beds, stoves and eating areas. Whereas this company performed their miracles with production vehicles, a few vehicle manufacturers produced their own version of a campervan. Most successful of these in terms of sales was VW, who continue to dominate that market.

Theresa expanded her search using the keyword 'campervan.' This provided a little further information, but of particular interest to her was the fact that there were specialist organisations that would hire out a campervan for a short period – anything from three days upwards. It occurred to her that she might take advantage of this to gain further knowledge and experience. In fact, she now wished she had realised this before she ventured off to Bircham, because it was now too late in the year, especially in view of her work situation. It was the type of activity best carried out when the nights were a little warmer, so she might re-visit the idea towards next summer.

The other subject she wanted to explore on the internet was the Green Man. She discovered that many churches, particularly in Norfolk, have a Green Man hidden somewhere within them, and sometimes not even well hidden. As she delved deeper into the subject, her imagination was heading more and more towards some pagan activity in her fictitious village of Burnham St Mary.

By now, the Earl Klugh CD had finished and Danny approached her once more. 'How are you getting on?' he asked.

It was obvious to Theresa that Danny was impatient for some of her attention, so she responded accordingly. 'I've made some progress, but I find I can only surf the internet for so long before I need a break. Shall we open a bottle of something?'

'Good idea,' Danny replied. 'You go and find something while I see to this CD.'

When she returned from the kitchen with the drinks, Danny pressed the 'play' button on the Hi-fi and took hold of Theresa's hand while the music started. He had selected one of their favourite tracks – *'Right By my Side'* by Stanley Clarke and George Duke, with a dreamy vocal by Gerald Alston. Danny held her close while they moved slowly to the music.

It had been a very long time since they had last danced together and both of them felt a little silly, but that didn't stop them holding each other closely and when the line *'how I need for you to be right by my side,'* came, Theresa leant her head on Danny's shoulder.

When the track finished, they stayed together in the middle of the room. 'Look at us,' Theresa said. 'Like a couple of adolescents!'

'Like a couple of adolescents in love!' Danny responded. 'I read something recently that sums up love. It was something to the effect that it's not a question of whether you love someone enough to live with them, but whether you can live without them. After a few months apart, I decided I can't live without you. The only thing that kept me going was the hope that we would get back together.'

Theresa hadn't moved from her position with her head on Danny's shoulder. 'Yes, I know,' she replied, but didn't add anything to this.

Danny suddenly uttered 'She was only the admiral's daughter, but she liked a naval encounter – especially with a great loss of seamen!'

Theresa gave a muffled laugh. 'Is that the humour for my book?'

'Yes. You said you wanted me to be thinking up ideas.'

'And how do I fit that into my book?'

'That's your area of expertise. I'm just the comedian. Anyway, are we going to have an early night?' Danny whispered.

'No. I think I want to sit down and watch some television together. Is there anything worth watching?' Theresa was testing Danny to make sure it wasn't just sex that he was missing. In any case, it was still far too early and there was still time for an 'early night.'

Danny let out a disappointed sigh, but didn't protest. 'I recorded something the other night I want you to see.' So they sat down with their wine in their usual positions in front of the television and Danny pressed a few buttons on the remote control. When the programme started, Theresa said 'This is *Fools and Horses*. We've seen all these.'

'Just wait a minute,' Danny replied.

He paused the programme when the title appeared. It was *Diamonds Are For Heather*.

'That's my title!' Theresa said.

'I thought you might recognise it,' Danny responded.

'I thought I'd invented it,' she said.

'You probably did, but unfortunately, so did someone else. You can still use it.'

'I was never intending to use it,' she replied. 'It does make you wonder if my other ideas have already been used. Did you record this just to show me that?'

'Yes. I thought you might see the funny side'

'So we're not really going to watch it, then?'

'We can if you like.'

'No, we've already seen them all at least twice. Isn't there a good drama we can watch?'

'Not that I can see. They don't seem to put on good dramas on a Friday night. I don't know why. There's *Have I Got News For You* at nine-thirty?'

'Ten minutes,' Theresa said looking at her watch. 'Just time to make some hot chocolate – then we'll have an early night. Has the bed been aired?'

'Well, I've been sleeping in it.'

'Does it need making?' she asked accusingly.

'Ah … I did say I left in a hurry this morning. I'll go and sort it out, now.'

'No, you make the chocolate. I'll make the bed. I haven't unpacked my case, yet.'

And a little while later, they had their early night.

In the morning, Theresa telephoned Judith to tell her that she would be vacating *Cherry Tree Cottage* at the end of the following week. Judith was pleased at this news as she had two bookings that she needed to fit in and was going to ask Theresa to help her accommodate them. Then she asked 'How is the writing?'

'Well, I've made a start. I've met a few interesting characters in the village and they've given me a few ideas.'

'Would I know them?' Judith asked.

'Well, there's a couple in the pub called Eddie and Millie. They're always bickering. Eddie keeps telling these appalling jokes and interrupting everyone else.'

'No, I don't think I know them.'

'Then there's this strange chap named Billy, who sits up the corner of the pub and stares at people.'

'Oh, I know him,' Judith said.' He is a bit scary. Have you met his brother Michael? He's really dreamy.'

For some reason, Theresa resented him being described as 'dreamy' and wanted to stick up for Billy, but decided not to. Instead, she replied 'No, I haven't met him, but Danny knows him. They work for the same company.'

'Of course they do. I'd forgotten that Danny's company was taken over.'

'Merged!' corrected Theresa.

'Whatever! You want to be careful of that Billy. Even Michael is a bit wary of him. You heard about his girlfriend dying, did you?'

'Yes, very tragic. He thought the world of her, you know.'

'That's as maybe, but he has got a temper on him – that's all I'm saying.'

Theresa considered that Judith was really trying to make an unsavoury point, but the subject changed and they made arrangements for returning the key.

Danny accompanied Theresa into Stamford and he wandered around town while she visited the opticians to get her spectacles repaired. She also visited the offices of Wadsworth & Associates, where she worked. There was only one person manning the fort that morning. This was Charles, recently graduated from Sheffield University and in his Part 1 'year out' before moving on to a further period at University in order to obtain his full RIBA qualification. Everyone else called him Charlie, but Theresa knew he preferred to be called Charles. She felt using his preferred name offered him more respect and lessened the chance of him being treated as an office junior, even though he was the most junior member of the team. She remembered her own early working years when she was expected to perform all the menial tasks and had to fight to gain meaningful experience.

Charles was able to give her more information about the new contract. It was primarily a development of luxury 4 and 5 bedroom detached houses, but with an obligation to provide a small number of 2 bedroom starter homes. Theresa was to concentrate her efforts on contract liaison and Charles would assist her.

It was a lovely mid-September day and as they drove home, Theresa said 'I fancy doing something this afternoon, before autumn takes over. Where can we go that doesn't involve too much travelling?'

Danny pondered the question for a while; then he had the answer.

'Lyveden New Bield,' he announced. 'It was about ten years ago when we went there and we said we'd go back sometime. That's not far away.'

'Oh, yes. I loved that place. It wasn't so much the building. It was those lovely moated gardens with the little mounds. I seem to remember that we rushed it last time, for some reason.'

'It was my bladder.' replied Danny. 'There were no toilets. But there are now – and a tea shop. We can stay as long as we want.'

'Let's do it. We'll have a quick sandwich when we get home and get out while the weather's nice.'

They had a delightful afternoon. In fact, they enjoyed the gardens so much that after a cup of tea and some delicious apple tart, they went round the grounds a second time, often clutching each other's hand, except when they parted to take a multitude of photographs, using telephoto shots and wide-angles from every direction.

As they sat together on a grassy bank, Danny said 'Shall we book a table at the Falcon, for tonight?'

'Or I can cook your favourite moussaka at home,' Theresa replied. 'That would be cheaper.'

'I want to celebrate our reconciliation.' Danny replied.

'We had a meal out on Tuesday.'

'But we weren't celebrating, then. We weren't fully reconciled at that point.'

'Well, you certainly reconciled me later that night,' Theresa joked.

'That was your lovely bowling ball buttocks,' Danny said with a lecherous look on his face.'

'Shh! People will hear you,' she said. 'You might not get a table this late in the day. The Falcon is usually well booked up on a Saturday.'

'Well, there's no harm in trying,' Danny said.

But Theresa was right in thinking they might not get a table, so they had their moussaka and a quiet evening at home with Danny watching 'Match of the Day' and everything getting back to normal. The following day, he wanted them to go out together, but Theresa insisted that they each had domestic chores that needed to be carried out and she duly presented Danny with a list of his. Both of them found getting back to 'normal' as being most satisfactory.

Chapter 10

Theresa was back at *Cherry Tree Cottage* just before lunchtime on Monday. After first enjoying a cup of coffee and then unpacking, she wandered down the village to the village shop where she picked up a few fresh supplies, including some more of their delicious ham. She felt strangely at home in this peaceful little village and happily exchanged greetings with two people in the shop as well as Mrs Thrower herself. The world seemed a better place than it was just a week ago.

And then it was down to work on her novel. She wanted to start on the first one or two chapters where she set the scene for Tess to embark on her journey in the campervan. Armed with her notes from the internet, Theresa could include details about the van, but was careful not to get too technical, in case a clever reader would pull her up over any possible error. But first, she wanted to include some background to the reasons for Tess to have ventured on such a trip. She also included a detailed description of Tess and her character. Theresa was at pains to ensure that the fictional Tess was nothing like herself, because she knew that writers often get accused of auto-biographical indulgences.

So Tess was a tall willowy blonde who didn't wear spectacles. She was amply endowed 'up top', but less so around the buttocks area. She was resourceful, bright and bubbly, although sometimes lacking in basic common sense. After all, who in their right mind would go off on their own in an old campervan? Her taste in men meant she was attracted to characters that were unafraid of danger. However, like Theresa, she did like men with a sense of humour.

One of the reasons for Tess' need to break away is that she was recently divorced from a man who was incapable of being faithful and this had shaken her world. Theresa toyed with the idea of making Tess' ex-husband bi-sexual or a latent gay, but she knew that Danny would read the novel at some point and she didn't know how he might react to this. He might well accept it for what it was – an original idea - but then again, he might not. It wasn't worth the risk.

Theresa worked on her novel for the rest of the day, stopping only for a quick lunch and to make regular cups of tea and by five o'clock, she had covered everything up to the point where she had left it last week, but now she had to make a few adjustments to her previous efforts to maintain continuity. She would do that after her tea. Everything was falling into place and she spent a further hour on the book before closing her laptop for the evening.

She felt thirsty, but had drunk enough tea and coffee for one day, so she thought she had earned something a little stronger. She was looking forward to seeing Millie and Eddie again, so she donned a coat and ventured out towards the *Bittern*. It was already dark and the lights from the pub seemed especially welcoming that evening.

As she entered the bar, there was no sign of Millie and Eddie, but what was even more surprising, was that Billy was not in his usual position. 'Have Millie and Eddie been here tonight?' she asked of Les, wondering if she might have already missed them.

'No, they're not back 'till tomorrow,' he replied. 'What will you have?'

'I'll have a cider, please,' she replied.

As she collected her drink, she looked around for a suitable seat where she could quickly consume it. Without Millie and Eddie, she didn't want to linger any more than necessary. The bar area was not too busy; just a couple of strangers by the window.

'Tess!' one of them called. She recognised the high-pitched voice, but Billy looked completely different. For one thing, he was wearing his spectacles. He was also wearing a sports jacket. She did not know his companion, but something about his appearance gave her an uneasy feeling. This was a man in love with himself. He was smartly dressed in a brown leather jacket and an orange shirt with a fairly large collar and two buttons left undone to reveal a few wisps of hairy chest and a gold chain. He had dark hair that was probably held in place with gel, although a few strands fell over his forehead. Theresa decided that those strands were placed there deliberately to give the impression of an active outdoor type.

'Come and join us,' Billy ordered. Theresa had little choice as the rest of the bar was devoid of customers, although she could hear voices from the dining area. She really didn't want to socialise with these two people, but there was no escape

'This is my brother Michael,' Billy announced, but Theresa already knew that. Who else could it have been from what she had heard of him?

Michael greeted her with a broad grin through immaculate white teeth. 'I am *so* pleased to meet you,' he said. The word "so" was emphasised in a seductive tone. The man was already coming on to her, she thought. 'I've heard so much about you. Carl talks very highly of you … but then, with his voice, he talks highly of everyone.'

Billy gave him a hard stare, but didn't say anything.

'And Daniel never stops talking about you. Tessa says this and Tessa does that. He was right about one thing. He said you were very attractive. I've always liked girls with glasses.'

Theresa knew that Danny didn't like being called Daniel. Only his mother used that name, so it seemed that Michael had a pet name for him, which annoyed her, as did the use of "Tessa." Absolutely no one had ever called her that – and certainly not Danny – and she couldn't imagine Danny telling anyone how attractive she was. Even if he felt like that, Danny just wouldn't say it – unless, perhaps he was asked the specific question 'Is your wife attractive?' Then he might say it.

'Come and sit beside me,' Michael added, patting a seat, but Theresa chose to sit opposite both of them. She was surprised at the complete absence of any local accent in Michael's voice when Billy's was completely 'country.'

She still hadn't been given the opportunity to speak, but at last she responded to Billy's request to join them by saying 'I can't stop for long, but I was very thirsty so I popped in for a quick one.'

'I like a quick one,' Michael replied, but Theresa wasn't in the mood for levity from this man, so she changed the subject.

'Thank you for buying my book,' she said to Michael. 'What did you think of it?'

'Yeah, it was good … not my sort of thing, to be honest … but, yeah. It was good.'

Theresa decided that he didn't really like it, but she knew that it probably wasn't to everybody's taste. At least he thought it was worth passing on to his brother.

'How's my good friend Danny?' Michael asked.

'He was very well when I left him this morning, thank you.' Theresa wondered if Michael knew about their separation. If so, he probably didn't know that they were back together again, so she had deliberately mentioned seeing Danny that morning. She was drinking her cider much quicker than she would normally do because she had no intention of lingering.

'That's good,' Michael responded. 'He's a great laugh … always greets us with a joke. He came in a few weeks ago and said he'd been dragged along to watch some ballet. He said if they're going to insist on the women dancing on tiptoe, wouldn't it be easier to get some taller girls?'

Theresa couldn't prevent herself from laughing. Because she hadn't seen Danny during that period, she hadn't heard that joke before.

'So it wasn't you that dragged him to a ballet?' Michael asked her.

'I don't think anyone could ever drag Danny to see a ballet,' she replied.

'Would you like a little bet?' Michael asked.

'I don't gamble,' Theresa replied.

'You will when you hear this. I bet that the next person to come in the bar has more than the average number of legs.'

Theresa had heard this one from Danny, so she wasn't about to get caught, but then she saw a couple of well-built men walking across the car park. Michael couldn't see them because his back was to the window.

'All right,' she said, 'as long as you can prove it to me.'

'Agreed,' said Michael. 'The loser buys a round of drinks.'

'I'm in, as well,' said Billy.

'You can't afford a round of drinks,' Michael replied. 'It's just me and Tess.'

Theresa resented Michael calling her Tess, but it was her own fault for trying to get 'into character,' which was meaningless now that the fictitious Tess was going to be a tall blonde with big breasts.

The first of the two men entered the bar. Billy strained his head around the corner to see who it was. 'It's Eric,' he said. 'He's definitely got two legs as he plays a lot of football. I used to play with him a few years back. I think you've lost your bet, Michael.'

'No,' replied Michael. 'Two is more than the average. If you take into account that some people have missing limbs and no one has three, that means the average is 1.98 or 1.99 or something like that. So someone with two legs has more than the average.'

'Yes, but how do I know he's got two legs?' asked Theresa. 'He might have a wooden leg for all I know.'

'But Billy has just told you he plays football,' Michael replied.

'The bet was that you had to prove it to me. Are you going to ask him to show me his legs?'

'I can't do that. He'll think I'm mad.'

'Well, you've lost the bet, then.'

Michael huffed and then said 'I was going to buy a round of drinks anyway. What will you have, Tess?'

'Not for me, thank you. I'll be off now.' By now, she had finished her cider.

'You can't go yet. Have another drink,' he insisted.

'No, really. One cider is enough for me.'

'Well, have a short, then.'

'I don't drink spirits,' she replied.

'Have a glass of wine. You can't go yet.'

'All right, I'll have a medium white wine – just a small one.'

While Michael was at the bar ordering the drinks, Billy leaned over to Theresa and said 'I got some great news. I'm gonna git a motor bike. Michael knows this chap who's gitting a motor and he needs rid of the bike. Michael's gonna lend me the money to pay for it and git it on the road. I'll be able to find a job somewhere.'

'That's great news, Billy. I do hope it works out for you.'

Michael returned with the drinks. Despite specifically asking for a small white wine, he presented her with a large one. She didn't mention it. He was either attempting to get her intoxicated or trying to impress her with his largesse, but Billy now had a full pint of ale in front of him, so it could have been the latter. Billy said 'Thanks mate' and eagerly took a first gulp.

Michael only had a half pint, so Theresa asked 'Are you driving tonight?'

'No, I'm staying at mum's. I just popped over for the weekend.'

'Is your wife with you?'

'No, she's at Taverham looking after the kids.'

'Where's Taverham?'

'It's a little village just outside Norwich,' Michael replied. Then it went a little quiet and Michael suddenly asked 'Have you heard about my tattoo?'

'No, why would I know about your tattoo?' Theresa replied in a puzzled tone.

'Because it's special.'

'Oh, tha's special,' piped in Billy with a huge grin on his red face.

'Well, what is it?' asked Theresa in a bored voice. She really wasn't interested in anyone's tattoo. In her opinion, she had yet to see a tattoo that actually improved a person's appearance. As for those footballers who covered their arms with tattoos, it just highlighted that they didn't know how to spend their exorbitant earnings.

'It's a bowling ball,' replied Michael in a tone that he felt would amaze anyone, except that Theresa still wasn't very impressed.

'Do you do a lot of ten-pin bowling, then?' she asked.

'Not really. It's because some people have described my buttocks as "bowling ball glutes." The tattoo is on my right cheek.'

Theresa was halfway through taking a swig of her wine, but stopped mid gulp and nearly choked. Michael felt this was because she was astounded by the thought of his wondrous adornment – or possibly intrigued by his impressive glutes, but that wasn't the reason at all. He had used a phrase very close to the one that Danny had used to describe her own buttocks. Was this just a coincidence?

'Do you want to see it?' Michael asked with a smug look on his face.

'No!' replied Theresa with a mixture of disgust and hatred.

'Your Danny's seen it. He made a joke about finding the correct finger holes.'

'When did Danny see it?' she asked.

'Um … let's see. That would be in the changing room when we played squash together.'

'Danny doesn't play squash!' Theresa responded accusingly. She was getting angry, not only at this topic of conversation, but also at the lies that Michael was now telling.

'Oh … not squash, then. That must have been someone else. I think it must have been when we went for a swim in his hotel in Norwich. It's a great tattoo. Are you sure you don't want to see it?' Other people might have squirmed at having been caught out with a lie, but Michael took it in his stride.

Theresa wanted to give a sarcastic answer, but her mind was in turmoil, so all she could say was 'Another time, perhaps,' which was totally the wrong thing to say to someone who thinks every woman is after his body. The reaction from Michael was that sickly but perfect smile.

She finished her wine much quicker than she wanted to and announced that it was time for her to be getting back. Billy said 'It's dark out there. I'll walk you back to your cottage.'

'No, it's all right,' she replied. 'It's no darker than when I came out, so I'm sure I'll manage to find my way.'

But by now, Billy had also gulped down the remains of his drink and Michael quickly followed suit and he insisted on accompanying them both, so Theresa was left with little option, but she didn't hang about and they followed a few feet behind. There was no further conversation before they all reached *Cherry Tree Cottage*.

Billy and Michael said a cheerful 'Goodnight.' Theresa's response was muted but polite.

Chapter 11

Theresa wanted to take her mind of events, so she sat down to watch some television. As she didn't have a TV guide, she scrolled through the channels. The Freeview reception in this part of the country wasn't brilliant and the choice was therefore very limited. She'd already missed the start of *Doc Martin* and there wasn't a 'plus 1' option available on this set so she switched to a documentary that had also already started, but gave up after fifteen minutes and went into the kitchen to make a mug of hot chocolate. She was very pleased that she had packed some chocolate digestives.

Just as the kettle was coming to the boil, she heard a noise behind her. Someone was in the house! She felt panic surging through her. She looked round for a weapon and found the breadknife.

'Hello Tess,' she heard and Michael appeared behind her at the kitchen door.

'How the Hell did you get in? I locked that door!' Theresa's voice must have sounded a little hysterical, which was hardly surprising.

'Judith gave me a key. We're very good friends, me and Judith. I often pop in when she's here.'

'You and Judith?' Theresa was trying to control her panic. He may not have been a violent burglar breaking into her cottage, but she guessed that his motives were not honourable. He had entered without an invitation and she wanted him gone. What sort of person enters a person's house with a key when he knows she could have answered a knock at the door?

'Get out! You've no right to use that key when someone else is staying here.'

'It's only me, Tess. We have unfinished business.'

'You don't have any business here. Now get out or I'll call the police.' She was now brandishing the breadknife, although she knew she wouldn't actually use it.

'Calm down. I'm not going to hurt you. Put that knife down before you hurt someone.'

'The only person who is going to get hurt is you. Now get out!'

Michael walked calmly towards her and held his hand out. 'Come on. Give me the knife.'

Theresa nervously waved the knife back and forth, but he still came forward and then quickly grabbed her arm before she knew it. She didn't expect him to be that fast. He gently prised the knife from her fingers and laid it on the kitchen table. 'That was silly,' he said. 'I only came here to talk.'

'You could have knocked on the door like normal people do,' she replied, breathlessly.

'I didn't want to stand on the doorway attracting attention.'

'Well, I'd like to attract attention!'

'A married woman comes into a pub on her own. What was I to think? Then you let me buy you a drink. I know you're only playing hard-to-get, but we might not get another chance.'

'I'm a happily married woman and you're a married man. Go home to your wife!'

'My wife understands that I need to do this.'

'Then your wife is a fool! If you carry on with this stupidity, it will amount to attempted rape.'

'But you were in the pub accepting drinks off me. You were heard to say that you would like to see my tattoo another time. That sounds like you were leading me on.'

All the time, his voice was soft and attempting to sound seductive – like Barry White, but Theresa knew this situation called for drastic measures and she drew her knee up rapidly into his nether regions. She felt him flinch, but he still stood in front of her. It hadn't worked! It works on the television. Why hadn't it worked now? Perhaps he approaches these situations wearing a box. Now he was going to be angry about what she'd just done. But then his face altered colour and he looked like he was going to throw up. He doubled up and she pushed him over with her foot.

She ran towards the door, but there in the door stood Billy. 'Wha's happened?' he asked.

'Your perverted brother has just tried to rape me.'

'He wouldn't have raped you,' Billy replied, 'but I had an idea he might try sumfent. He said he was going out for a walk, but Michael; he don't go for walks, so I guessed what he were about. He's got a bit of a problem, you see. He can't leave it alone. It's an obsession.'

By now, Michael was on his feet again, but still looking the worse for wear.

Theresa stared at him and said 'If you're that desperate, I'm sure you could find one of the village girls who might be impressed by your stupid tattoo - weirdo!'

'There's no girls in the village since Lynn died,' he gasped.

'How about one of the sheep, then?'

'For your information, it's all arable farming around here,' he muttered.

'Oh, so you have considered it?'

Billy grabbed Michael by the arm and pushed him out of the door.

'Wait a minute!' called Theresa. 'I want the door key off him. I don't want him coming back here – and he might try it on with some other tenants.'

'Gimme the key!' Billy demanded.

'It's my key. Judith entrusted it to me.'

'Well, you blew that trust,' Theresa said. 'Now hand it over. And I'll tell Judith why I wanted it back.'

Michael looked hurt at this. It probably meant he wouldn't be able to pop round to see Judith whenever he wanted. Billy shook him violently and Michael threw the key on the floor. They both left.

Theresa locked the door behind them, using Michael's key to ensure he had given her the correct one. For good measure, she drew the bolt across. She stood with her back against the door and breathed heavily, trying to recover herself.

Well, she wanted some adventure. She considered that she'd just had one. She wondered what would have happened if Billy hadn't come along. Good old Billy. She'd have to thank him when she saw him next.

This was the second Monday in a row that she had felt the need to bolt her door and each time it was one of the Bingham brothers causing her fear. She had come to realise that Billy was not a malevolent psychopath. The madness in their family was in his brother. In her opinion, he needed psychiatric help. She'd heard the term 'sex maniac' before, but never realised it might be a real affliction, if 'affliction' was the right word to use. She remembered reading that John F. Kennedy had a problem like this. The story she read said he would feel ill if he didn't have sex. Was that the way with Michael or was the story with JFK just sensational journalism?

When Theresa rose the next day, it was as though the events of the previous evening had all been a bad dream. Whilst in bed, she had spent the waking hours trying to make sense of it all and questioning whether she had done anything to encourage Michael in his behaviour. She decided that she hadn't, except for that one phrase – 'perhaps another time' – which would have been taken as a sarcastic put-down to most people, but Michael was obviously not 'most people.' He wouldn't have been able to accept a put-down. To him, anyone who could resist his charms was either a prick-teaser or a lesbian. She did eventually fall into a deep sleep, to be woken at dawn by the sun's rays angling through her bedroom window.

At this time of year, fine days had to be grasped, so she decided she would head for the coast to explore parking options for a campervan. Many other people would have withdrawn into themselves after her experience, but Theresa felt the need to escape from this village for a while – and away from the Binghams. Not only that, but once this week was over, she would have to return to the drudgery of day to day commuting and traffic queues in Stamford.

She was busy washing up the breakfast things when she heard a knock at the door. She could think of no reason why anyone might be calling and memories of the previous evening filled her with fresh trepidation. As she unbolted the door, but before turning the key in the lock, she called 'Who is it?'

'S'only me – Carl … er, Billy.' Of course Theresa had already recognised his distinctive voice.

'Are you alone?' she asked.

'Yes, totally alone,' came the reply. So Theresa opened the door. So much for getting away from the Binghams, but she owed Billy and wanted to thank him again. He was still wearing his spectacles. 'I just wanted to come round and say sorry about Michael and make sure you're or'right.'

'Yes, I'm all right now, thank you. But as you can see from my precautions, I'm still a little wary about visitors.'

'Well, I won't stay. I just wanted to say sorry and let you know that Michael's gone home now. I won't keep you.'

'No, come in, please. I wanted to tell you how grateful I was to see you last night. I don't know what would have happened if you hadn't turned up. Can I get you a coffee or a cup of tea?'

'Yes, please. I'll have whatever yor havin'. You know wooden have actually hurt you. He were just tryin' it on.'

'You weren't here just before I kneed him. I don't think he was going to take "no" for an answer. I know you want to stick up for him; being your brother and all, but I really felt I needed to stop him.' Billy shrugged his shoulders. 'There was one thing he said that made me think. He said there were no other girls in the village since Lynn died. Did he ever try it on with Lynn?'

'No! Absolutely not! He wooden dare. He knows how much she meant to me ... no! No!'

But Theresa could see Billy was just thinking about the possibility for the very first time. She poured them both a mug of coffee.' How do you have it?' she asked, but Billy took a minute for the question to register.

When they were half-way through their drinks, Theresa said 'I said I'd let you look at the extension. As you can see, we made the kitchen bigger and added an upstairs bathroom above it. It's just an ordinary bathroom – no fancy fittings or anything.' Theresa didn't want to take him upstairs. It didn't seem right and proper. 'And, of course, we used local brick and flint on the outside walls so it all blends in. We put the central heating in, of course and a new fireplace. The old one was really too small.'

Billy looked around to take it all in. 'I wonder what Aunt Lesley would have made of it? In the winter, she had to huddle round a small coal fire. None of the other rooms had any heating, although she did have a small one-bar electric fire that smelt of burnt dust. She never had any children, so me and Michael were often invited 'round, particularly Sundays. She all'ays had fish on Sundays, so the house stank, but we never minded. She liked to play cards with us – had a pot of pennies so's we didn't gamble our own money. I really miss Aunt Lesley ... really do.'

'Was she married?' Theresa asked seeing the sadness in his face.

'Yeah, but Uncle Tom died in the seventies – 'ad a 'eart attack ... real sudden. She never got over it. I fink I know how tha' feels.'

Theresa decided to change the subject to lift their spirits. 'Do you go to the church?'

'Not inny more. I did when I were younger.'

'Do you know anything about the church?'

'What do you want to know?' Billy replied with another question.

'Well, when I can visit for one thing.'

'I think it's open Sunday mornings, but tha's about it. – oh, and weddin's an' funerals, but we don't have many of them.'

Theresa looked disappointed. 'Does anyone have a key if I wanted to look around?'

Billy looked thoughtful for a minute before answering 'They must have, 'cause the ladies do the flowers ready for Sundays.'

'Who are the ladies?'

'Millie is one of them.'

'I'll try to speak to Millie, then. I haven't seen her for a few days. Are you going to the pub, tonight?'

'Spec so. I usually do. Will I see you there?'

'No. Your brother was right about one thing. A married woman shouldn't go into a pub on her own. If you do see Millie, will you tell her about my interest in the church?'

'Ar, if I sees her.' Billy stood up. 'I'd best be arf. Thanks for the coffee.'

'You're more than welcome – and thanks again for saving me last night.'

'Don't know about savin' you, but I'm glad I was there.'

Chapter 12

Theresa checked her atlas to establish her route to Blakeney. There was a satnav in her car, but she loved to look at maps and, as in this case, she would often choose the most interesting route to reach her destination. She knew that Norfolk abounded with pretty villages which often get neglected in favour of the easy option of heading straight for the coast, not that there was a direct route from where she was. One place she had often wanted to visit, but had yet to do so, was Walsingham. The last time that she and Danny had considered visiting was one Easter when they knew the pilgrims would be about and they didn't fancy filling in an insurance claim form for colliding with one of them. After all, the pilgrims were unlikely to have insurance cover themselves and those crosses can be very difficult to avoid.

She discovered that there are two Walsinghams – Great Walsingham and Little Walsingham. Surely Great Walsingham would be the one she wanted, so that's where she headed, only to find that the main attractions were to be found in Little Walsingham. She parked her car and explored the village. The many interesting buildings in the area were, for her, spoiled by the numerous souvenir shops selling religious paraphernalia, but that was only to be expected in a village where the main centre of attraction was a holy shrine.

By now, it was lunchtime and while visiting the grounds of the Shrine, she discovered a delightful little restaurant where she had a delicious quiche salad accompanied by some real lemonade. Not being particularly religious herself, Theresa still enjoyed the tranquillity of the gardens within the grounds of the shrine and watched as others quietly strolled around, occasionally pointing out something to their companions and whispering reverently. She felt guilty that Danny wasn't with her. She shouldn't be out enjoying herself, but she had a lot to think about and this was the ideal place for contemplation.

First of all, she had to decide whether she would tell Danny about Michael's advances. After due consideration, she decided not. For one thing he might react violently towards Michael – no, not "*might*" – "*would*." How could he not? He did love her and would want to protect her – and then he might get into trouble himself. Despite what Billy had said, she was convinced that Michael would have tried to force himself upon her.

And then she still felt uncomfortable about the reference to bowling balls and the fact that Danny had apparently seen Michael's glutes. Of course, Michael could have been lying about that, but she could imagine Danny making a little joke about finger holes. She decided that she would confront Danny about this, but she would try to do it tactfully. She didn't want Danny to feel she still had irrational feelings of jealousy – even if she did!

She closed her eyes and drank in the tranquillity of the gardens hoping all this silliness would go away.

As Theresa drew into the outskirts of Blakeney she found a free car park. Having been married to Danny for fifteen years, it had become second nature to favour a short walk over a car park fee, but of interest to her was that the car park sign confirmed that overnight parking was not allowed for caravans and campervans. She carefully read the sign to ensure she could actually park there for free and that there were no hidden clauses. She didn't want to return to find her car clamped because she was only allowed ten minutes to use the toilets or some other silly condition, but there really were no catches. A free car park is, after all, unusual for a seaside resort. She remembered a trip to Polperro where they had no choice but to pay a large amount to park on the outskirts of the village and then had a long walk to get to the harbour, although it was mostly a pleasurable walk.

And, now, a short stroll did indeed take her down to the attractive harbour of Blakeney. She loved this village. It had a charm all of its own. The tide was out, which gave it a completely different feel to when the creek was full, but it was still every bit as charming. Many of the little dinghies were stranded on the mud, but a few could still be seen reflecting their masts in the shallow water in the middle of the creek. She fetched her compact camera from her bag to capture the scene, but found her trip to Lyveden New Bield had drained the battery. She had taken photographs on previous trips to Blakeney, but the harbour never looked exactly the same – different tide conditions; different light; different time of day; even, like now, a different time of year.

She walked past the luxury hotel complex that dominates the harbour frontage and forms an easily recognised backdrop that seems to occupy the view from any direction. Whenever Danny saw this building, he would boast of having stayed there – admittedly for a team building course at company expense (a waste of time as far as he was concerned) – but at the same time, he would resent anyone who could afford their tariff. He wasn't a socialist, but he had always felt the need to watch the pennies. He once joked that when he was young, if he needed a new pair of shoes, his mother told him to visit the local swimming pool. It wasn't true, of course. Danny was as honest as the day is long. Theresa also remembered another of his little witticisms told at the same time. His mother used to get his clothes from the Army & Navy store. The kids at school couldn't understand why he went to school dressed as an admiral.

She did miss Danny and wished he was with her. It seemed unfair that they had been separated for so long and just when they were reconciled, it was in the middle of this working holiday. She might decide to go home a day or two early. She would have liked to have called him, but her phone still wasn't getting a decent signal.

She continued her walk to the harbour car park, which was far busier than the free park. Obviously some people would rather pay a fee than walk a few yards. This was a pay and display area, but although it was administered by the council, it was free to National Trust members. However, Theresa remembered she had handed her membership card to Danny for safe keeping when they went to Lyveden and his vehicle had the car sticker, so if she had used this car park, she would have been forced to pay which would have been very frustrating with her being a Trust member. Again a sign said no overnight camping, so that confirmed her thoughts, which was why the fictional Tess was going to park in a field. Gaining this information was her main reason for this little excursion – at least, that's what she told herself.

A delightful fifteen minute stroll along the coast path swept away all the painful memories of the previous night. Although this was still Norfolk, it was a different world. An egret could be seen stabbing its beak into the water's edge about fifty yards away. Terns swooped and called to each other. Ringed plovers scuttled across the mudflats searching for food and all the time, there was the steady clanging of the yachts' rigging along the edge of the creek. Theresa could easily have stayed longer and walked further but she decided that she needed a cup of tea. So she turned around and as she looked back to the village, she realised that she had walked further than intended. Back at the harbour, she looked for a nice little tea shop, but there was none to be seen. There were the two hotels, which would probably serve tea and there was a pub, but she wouldn't have felt comfortable on her own. So she ignored them all while she wandered up the High Street, past the shops selling paintings and other various items that were of no interest to her at that time. Surely, there would be a tea shop somewhere along this street, but she was coming to the last of the shops and still nothing. Someone could be making a small fortune by opening such a business in this village. Another fifty yards or so and she would be back on the main coast road. With tired reluctance, she turned around to head back down the way she had come, but walking from a different direction enabled her to see a sign she had missed on the way up. It said lunches were served from 12.00 to 3.00 p.m.; afternoon teas from 3.00. It was a secluded hotel, but it looked expensive. Never mind – she felt like treating herself.

She seemed to be the only customer and she wondered if the tea room was actually open. She looked at the menu which didn't actually mention a pot of tea – just afternoon tea with a selection of scones and cakes. The tables were all laid out with full cutlery and fine linen napkins. She began to suspect that this establishment would not welcome a single order of a pot of tea for one. She wouldn't mind a biscuit or two, but cake and scones would dull her appetite for the meal she had half prepared before leaving the cottage. After a few minutes, a casually dressed man appeared to take her order.

'Can I just have a pot of tea, please?'

'Of course – nothing with it?' His voice was quite refined but friendly.

'No, just the tea, please.'

Theresa felt a little uncomfortable sitting on her own just staring out of the window, but the man soon re-appeared with a set of quality crockery and a teapot. 'Are you on holiday?' he asked.

'Well, a working holiday, you could say. I'm up here for a few weeks while I work on my next novel.'

'You're a writer? How wonderful!' He sounded genuinely appreciative. 'Would I have heard of you?'

'My name is Theresa Finbow. My last book was called *Happy is a Grumpy Road.* I doubt whether you will have heard of it. It hasn't sold as well as I'd hoped.'

'What's it about?' he asked.

Theresa gave him a brief outline of the book.

'I like that sort of thing,' he remarked. 'How can I get hold of a copy?'

'Well, you can go to any bookshop and they should be able to order it. You can buy it online from all the usual sources. Or …' she hesitated for effect, 'I just happen to have a brand new copy in my bag' and she duly fetched it out for him.

'If I buy this, will you sign it for me?' he asked, fingering it as though he had just found a valuable antique.

'Of course I will. I do hope you enjoy reading it.' She asked his name, which was Michael (not her favourite name at that moment), but she inserted a short message and added her signature. She had to remember to use her author signature rather than her usual married name, which she used for signing cheques and legal documents.

Michael stood talking to her for a few minutes, mainly discussing the merits of North Norfolk, while she drank her tea.

When she stood up to leave, he shook her hand and thanked her again. She said 'Not at all. That's the first time I've bought a cup of tea and made a profit.'

Theresa walked back down to the harbour with a spring in her stride. She always felt elated when she had sold a book. It wasn't the money. It was the thought that someone would take some time out of their lives to read her work and hopefully it would bring them some pleasure. Just to cheer her even more, the tide was now coming in, so the scene in the harbour was transformed and she could enjoy the revised views all over again. She lingered by the creek for a few minutes, watching as the tide gradually floated some of the dinghies which earlier had been stuck in the mud.

For most of the afternoon, all thoughts of the previous evening had been banished to the dark recesses of her mind, but as she drove back to Bircham, they re-emerged. She wanted to see Millie to find out about visiting the church and she didn't know if she could rely on Billy to relay her message, so the only way to talk to her was to visit the pub again.

Chapter 13

Throughout the evening, Theresa contemplated a quick visit to the *Bittern,* but every time she made preparations to go, feelings of panic came over her. Billy had said that Michael had gone home, but that didn't prevent him from coming back again. So she left her door locked and bolted all evening. She tried to tell herself that she was being irrational, but she realised that she was, in fact, being perfectly sensible.

The sea air and the walking had exhausted her, so she decided on a comparatively early night, but as she filled the kettle for her hot chocolate, she heard a knock at the door. This was the second time that day that someone had called on her and she was in no more of a hurry to answer this time.

'Who is it?' she called through the door.

'It's Millie,' was the response.

Relief swept over her as Theresa hurriedly unshot the bolt and turned the key.

'You're a bit nervous,' Millie said as the door opened. 'Are you expecting the Spanish Inquisition?'

Theresa felt a bit silly, but she just replied 'I'm all alone in a strange place. It doesn't hurt to be careful. Come in, please.'

Eddie was standing there as well and she ushered them both into her sitting room. 'I was just making a cup of hot chocolate. Can I get you both something?'

'Do you have any unleaded coffee?' Eddie asked as he entered.

'I'm afraid not. I've got some at home, but that's no use now. My father-in-law has to have decaff when he comes round due to his blood pressure. He always calls it decapitated coffee. There used to be a comedian who used that line a lot. He said he didn't like a head on it.'

'Johnny Casson,' said Eddie.

'That's right; it was – a very funny chap.'

'Chocolate would be lovely, thank you,' said Millie. 'We always have a mug of chocolate before we turn in for the night.'

'How was your break?' Theresa asked while she busied herself in the adjoining kitchen.

Before Millie could say anything, Eddie had dived in. 'Bloody awful. Our daughter hasn't got the room to put us up, so we checked into this little hotel. We were told that breakfast were included. It turned out to be one of them there continental breakfasts. Bloody waste of time – fruit juice, cereals and yoghurt! I don't see the point of yoghurt. It's made wiv stuff that's gone off and 'as bacteria added. Bacteria! Who wants bacteria added to their food? I don't know how my stomach survived.'

Millie responded. 'You wouldn't even try the yoghurt, so you can hardly talk about surviving.' We had a lovely time, thanks, love.'

But Eddie wasn't finished. 'My son-in-law, when 'e wanted to marry our Liz, he came up to me to ask for her hand in marriage. I said "Can you support a family?" He said "Can't you support yourself?"'

Millie had heard all of Eddie's jokes before so she joined Theresa in the kitchen, where Theresa was just popping the foil on a fresh jar of chocolate, but Eddie hadn't finished and he followed Millie. 'I like that sound of popping fresh jars of coffee and chocolate. Mind you, I've been banned from the supermarket!'

'You've got a lovely laugh,' Millie said to Theresa, who, unlike Millie, was enjoying all of Eddie's little quips.

'That's what Danny says. He says it makes him want to try to be funny all the time.'

'We used to be like that,' said Millie. 'But after a while you get fed up with the same old material – in more ways than

104

one! Anyway, Billy told me you wanted to speak to me about the church. Is that right?'

'Yes, I wanted to have a look 'round some time, if that's possible? I hear you sometimes go in to arrange the flowers.'

'Yes, we do that on a Wednesday afternoon. I've got a key if that doesn't suit.'

'No, tomorrow afternoon will be just great. That will probably be my only chance to look around. I think I'm going home on Thursday. I have to be back at work next week.'

'Will you be coming back?' Millie asked.

'Not this year. We're going to be very busy at work. They wanted me to go back this week, but I insisted on a few more days over here.'

'I expect you'll be glad to get back to Danny. Do you have any children?'

'No. With all the studying to be an architect and forging careers, we never got round to that.'

'Is that what Danny is, then – an architect?'

'No, that's me. Danny's in IT.'

'You don't hear about female architects, do you?'

'There are a few, but I'm the only one in our office.'

Well, we'll be very sorry to see you go, won't we Eddie?'

'Aye, we will, lass. I've been reading some more of your book. It's very enjoyable. I like the bit about the old man having irritable bowel syndrome brought on by being a grumpy old man and his daughter saying she expected him to develop a grumbling appendix. I think I may have sold one or two copies for you.'

'How have you managed that?' Theresa asked.

'Well, lass here, dragged me along t'art gallery. Well I can't do with all that, especially with my knees. So I left her to it while I sat down to read it on bench in one of them galleries. This elderly lady sat down beside me for a rest and asked what it were that I were reading. I showed it to her, like and said how good it were and she made a note to look out for it. And our son-in-law has got one of them kindling devices, so he said he might download it.'

'Why, thank you, Eddie. I need all the sales I can get. And I will miss you both, by the way – even Eddie's jokes!' She meant this even if she did prefer Danny's jokes, but many of Eddie's were one-liners which were much more suitable to steal for her writing.

Eddie treated this compliment as an invitation. 'I've been suffering with pins and needles. Do you think I should try acupuncture?' he said.

'I'm sure Tess was only being polite,' Mille said, without laughing, but Eddie hadn't finished.

'Brain surgeons,' he said. 'You have to take your hat off to them.'

'Are you a churchgoer, then?' Millie asked, desperate to stop Eddie's jokes.

'No, not really, but I do love the old buildings - especially cathedrals. I'm told there's a green man in this church and I want to have a look for it.'

'I've never heard of that, have you Eddie?'

'I 'ave heard of the green man. It's a pagan symbol of fertility, in't it? I can't see why there would be one of them in a church.'

'Apparently,' replied Theresa, 'lots of churches have one – usually well hidden. I'll find out tomorrow how well hidden!'

Millie said 'I was a bit surprised when Billy approached us in the pub. He's never tried to speak to us before. He seemed different – more sociable, even.'

Theresa thought about this for a few seconds before asking 'Was he wearing his glasses?'

'Yes, he was, now that you come to mention it.'

'I bet that makes a difference. I find if I'm not wearing mine, it's harder to join in with people's conversation. I think it's something to do with not being able to read people's expressions. I didn't particularly want to go to the pub tonight, so I did ask Billy to tell you I wanted to talk to you about the church.'

'Well, he did that,' Millie added, 'and he asked us if we'd had a nice break. I've never known him to do something like that before. His brother would, but not Billy.'

'Do you know his brother very well?' Theresa asked.

'I know enough. I don't like him. There's something shifty about him. They're two completely different characters – not like brothers at all.'

Theresa resisted the temptation to tell her about their parentage. It was something told in confidence.

'He'd shag a dog if it kept its mouth shut!' announced Eddie.

'Eddie! Theresa doesn't want to hear language like that!' Millie said, giving him a very hard stare.

'It's all right, Millie. I think I've heard worse talk than that. In fact, Eddie did well to say "shag." And I've heard similar comments about Michael. I thought Billy was a bit scary when I first saw him – the way he sat on his own, staring, but now I think he's probably all right.'

'Billy's harmless – although I hear he has a temper.'

While they all drank their chocolate, they continued with some friendly small talk, which included Eddie's views on religion ('lot of mumbo jumbo!') and Theresa and Millie agreed to meet in the church the following afternoon.

When Theresa arrived at the church, the ladies were all busy taking out the flowers from the previous week and Millie introduced the other ladies, one of whom was Mrs Fitheridge. After exchanging some pleasantries, Theresa said 'Don't mind me. I'll keep out of your way while you're all working,' and she started to look around, mainly to find the green man, but also to admire the building. She could hear Mrs Fitheridge chattering all the time. 'These chrysantheums are still in good condition. Does anyone have any objectives if I take them for my front room?'

It was a very pretty church, but quite small so Theresa didn't think it would take her long to find the object. Half an hour later, she was still looking and decided to ask the other ladies if they knew of its whereabouts. None of them did. Mrs Fitheridge was busy arranging her coronations and her Friesians.

Theresa was starting to feel very frustrated. She'd looked at the pews, the font, each of the doors, all the wood panelling and the pulpit. She strained her neck to scan every square foot of the fading painted ceiling, having remembered that the dog walker had told her to look upwards.

And then she found it. There were a series of grotesques on the capitals of all the columns either side of the main aisle. These were very similar to those alternating with the gargoyles on the outside of the church. Theresa knew that a gargoyle served to disgorge rainwater from roof guttering, whereas a grotesque was purely decorative, although usually not very decorative at all, since they were, as the name suggests, grotesque. All of the interior grotesques were hideous depictions of the human head, often appearing to be in agony, but the green man was made even more hideous by the branches and twigs growing out of every orifice of the man's head and wrapping themselves around him. Unlike the other grotesques, this face seemed to be smiling. You could only spot it if you were walking away from the altar whilst looking upwards. It was an incredible piece of carving and Theresa marvelled at the sculptor's skill, but knew that if she had come across this at night time, it could easily give her nightmares. She wondered how many brides had gazed at it on their way back from the altar.

She started to imagine various scenarios where the fictitious Tess might come across a green man, not necessarily in a church, but perhaps in some other old building – a manor farm building might be a possibility. Tess might discover that Toby's evil rival was mixed up in some kind of pagan coven, if there is such a thing. Druids and the occult often feature in popular fiction, so there was more food for thought.

Millie could tell from the delighted look on Theresa's face that she had found her object and joined her to look at it. 'What a horrible sight,' she said, as the other ladies joined them. 'Looks a bit like Eddie that time he tried to grow a beard,' she added and they all laughed, before remembering where they were, muting their enjoyment.

The next day, Theresa called in on Mrs Fitheridge to return the key. 'Oh, what a pity,' Mrs Fitheridge said. 'I like to see the cottage being used. It only ever seems to get booked during the school holidays. I think it's a little too far from the coast, you know. People don't want to travel too far, do they? I had a couple here earlier this year – I think they came up from London – they'd seen the Broads on the telly. So they thought that as Bircham was in Norfolk, it would do, but they had no idea where the Broads are. They asked me the best place to go. Well, do you know, I've never been to the Broads myself – lived in Norfolk for over fifty years and never been. So I thought, and I said that I thought Wroxham was on the Broads. They asked me where that was. I said I didn't know – I'd never been. So they tried to enter the name into their satnat and off they went. Well, they ended up in the middle of nowhere near Downham Market in a tiny little place called Roxham – without the 'W' – nowhere near the Broads. They didn't have any maps, you see. They came up from London using their satnat and imagined that would do for them. Anyway, they turned around and drove up though Swaffham, hoping they would see some road signs to the Broads, but, of course, none of the road signs mention the Broads as a location, do they? Anyway, to cut a long story short, they ended up in Holkham and had a very nice afternoon on the beach. When they came back, they told me they didn't like

Roxham and wondered if I'd got the name wrong and it should have been Holkham. Then they said they didn't realise that the Broads were by the sea. I ask you. Anyway, I lent them some maps and some books and they did eventually find the Broads. They went to a little place called Horsey Mere. They had a nice boat ride and said they saw some March Harriers and some Grey Herrings.'

Theresa eventually got a word in. 'Yes, we went there a few years ago – a lovely place. Can I ask you a question? Does anyone have a spare key to the cottage?'

'Only me and Judith,' came the reply. 'Why do you ask?'

Theresa wasn't going to tell her the real reason for asking, so she lied. 'As I was driving over on Monday, I was nearly here when I suddenly had this horrible thought that I'd left the key at home – but I hadn't. But I wondered what I would do if I had.'

'Yes, I do keep a spare just in case someone loses one.'

Theresa decided not to pursue the matter any further. It was clear that Mrs Fitheridge didn't know about Michael's key. 'I mustn't keep you any longer,' she said. 'I need to get off.' She was anxious that Mrs Fitheridge might start another one of her monologues and really did want to be on her way. *Cherry Tree Cottage* now held too many bad memories.

Theresa was determined that her need to confront Danny about some of Michael's statements wouldn't lead to a big falling out, but she knew it would eat away at her if she didn't tackle the matter. Her diplomatic skills would be put to the test. She had driven home early enough to prepare a lovely lasagne for their evening meal. When Danny returned from work, she greeted him with a big hug and a lingering kiss.

She had heard that women who had been sexually assaulted could be so traumatised by the experience that they would no longer welcome intimate contact, but this didn't seem to be the case with her. In fact, at that moment, she craved it. Perhaps a near-miss doesn't count.

'I've missed you,' she said.

'I should think so, too,' he replied, pulling her close to him. 'I wasn't expecting you until tomorrow. This is a nice surprise.'

Theresa smiled at him. 'I would have called, but I couldn't get a signal.'

'I can smell something nice. What is it?' Danny asked.

'It's probably me,' she said, while still holding him.

'Have you being putting a touch of garlic behind your ears?' he said with a big grin.

'Is that what it takes to capture your heart?'

'It's too late for that. You captured my heart many years ago.'

'Well it's nearly ready. Do you want to change out of your suit while I serve it up?'

'Will it keep? I want to feast on something else, first.'

'No, it will spoil. Now, go and get changed.'

Danny was feeling totally full up after a second helping, so he flopped down on the settee and put his other appetites on hold for a while. While he was in a contented mood, Theresa saw her opportunity and sat beside him. 'I saw your mate Michael this week.'

Danny suddenly seemed more alert and looked up. 'Where was that?'

'He was with his brother in the pub. He'd spent the weekend with his parents.'

'Did you speak to each other?' Danny's tone was tinged with concern.

'Yes, the bar was empty, so when Billy invited me to join them, I didn't feel I had any choice. He said some interesting things.'

'What Michael or Billy?'

'Michael – Billy doesn't say a lot.' Theresa was determined

to make this sound like idle chit-chat before she got to the matters that concerned her. 'He kept wanting to talk about his tattoo.'

'Not his bloody tattoo? He's obsessed with it.'

'Have you seen it?' Theresa asked.

'Of course I've seen it. He was flashing it about the bedroom that night we shared a room – kept asking if I wanted to feel it. I thought he was just a bit drunk at first and laughed it off - told him I might get the wrong finger hole or something like that. But then, he got more serious and told me he had an enormous erection and that I had to help him with that. That's when I told him to leave. I felt really angry, but I didn't fancy getting violent with a naked man.'

'... especially one with an enormous erection,' added Theresa. 'Couldn't you just kick him in the balls? That's what I would have done.'

'The thought never crossed my mind.' Danny said. 'I just wanted him to go away.'

'I can't say I blame you,' said Theresa, still trying to keep the conversation as light as possible, but all the time, remembering her own experience with Michael. 'Did you ever go for a swim at the hotel pool?'

'No. Why?'

'Because Michael said that was where you had seen his tattoo. Although he wasn't sure if it might have been in the changing rooms when you played squash together.'

'We never played squash nor went for a swim. Perhaps he just didn't think you knew about sharing a room and was trying to protect me. You didn't let his lies upset you, did you?'

'No, of course not. I could tell he was telling lies when he mentioned squash. I knew you don't like squash. However, I was a bit concerned that you'd use the term "bowling ball buttocks" about me and then he used a similar term.'

Danny sighed. 'Yes, I see. It seemed like a good expression, so I thought I could borrow it. I wouldn't have done if I'd know you were going to be subjected to that idiot's twaddle.'

Theresa had made her point and had to accept the explanation. So she just added 'Oh, well. He's not worth bothering about, is he?'

'The funny thing is,' said Danny, 'that most of the time he was good company. Up until that point, we had gotten on really well – strange bloke!'

Theresa had got the matter off her chest and now the two of them could get on with their lives without ever being bothered by Michael again.

Chapter 14

Theresa waited until Danny had left for work before she telephoned Judith to tell her that she had a key to return.

'You normally leave it with Mrs Fitheridge,' Judith replied.

'I left *my* key with Mrs Fitheridge, but this is Michael Bingham's key,' Theresa said and then proceeded to explain everything.

'That must have been terrifying for you,' Judith said when Theresa had finished her story. 'Did you tell Danny what happened?'

'No. I was afraid he might do something silly and get himself into trouble – and that's the only reason I didn't go to the police either. I hope you won't let that animal have your key back.'

'No, I won't. Although I have to say that he's never struck me like that. Are you sure you didn't lead him on in anyway?'

'Excuse me!' Theresa raised her voice angrily in reply. 'I happen to be happily married!'

'All right,' replied Judith.' It's just that I know Michael quite well and I can't imagine him behaving like that. I admit that he does have a voracious appetite, though'

Theresa didn't want to know how Judith would know about that. Judith had never really settled down with one man for very long. 'Anyway,' she added trying to calm herself, 'I need to get this key to you. Do you want to meet up for a coffee sometime?'

'That's going to be awkward at the moment. During the week, I'm busy commuting to the Smoke and at weekends, Selwyn comes up to stay with me.'

'Who's Selwyn?' Theresa enquired.

'He's my partner. He works in London with me. We've been seeing each other for about four months now.'

'This sounds serious?' Theresa said, knowing Judith's relationships seldom lasted much longer than this.

'Well, you know me. Easy come, easy go. We do have a lot in common. I tell you what. Why don't you and Danny come over for a meal this weekend? Then you can meet him. You've often said you'd like to see my place'

That was true. Judith had boasted of living in a house by the river in Godmanchester and Theresa had always felt envy whenever Judith had talked about it. Moreover, it would be beneficial for her and Danny to go out together. They hadn't seen much of their mutual friends during their separation. 'Yes, that sounds good. I think we're both free all this weekend.' So they arranged their visit for that Sunday.

Danny wasn't too enthusiastic about the invitation. He'd only met Judith once and didn't feel that she and he would ever form any kind of friendship. During that previous meeting, he had felt that Judith was constantly trying to impress Theresa with her material goods, such as her flashy car and her house by the river. What's more, Danny couldn't imagine getting on with anyone called Selwyn. Perhaps Selwyn was a bit of a 'balm-pot.' The thought reminded him of Norman Clegg in *The Last of the Summer Wine*. Cleggy always liked encountering a 'balm-pot' and relished the opportunity to make fun of him. With that in mind and because Judith was Theresa's friend, he magnanimously agreed to accompany Theresa and they made their way down the A1 to wonder at this marvellous house by the river; except that they discovered it wasn't actually by the river. It was a good walk away from the river, but Danny had to admit that it was a lovely situation. Not only was it within sight of the river, but it was also a short walk away from a lovely grassy meadow.

Danny parked the car in the road a few yards away from the property as Judith's driveway was filled with a brand new Range Rover Evoque and a two year-old Audi TT. 'If I get bored,' he said, as they walked towards the house, 'I can always go for a little stroll across the meadow – or visit the Chinese Bridge. I've always wanted to see that.'

'You won't get bored. That's an order!' Theresa said. She knew that Danny usually reacted to new people in one of several ways. If he found them interesting, he would, of course, engage them in meaningful conversation and be his usual humorous self. If he took a dislike to them, he would take the piss. If he found them to be show-offs, he would take the piss - and if he found them boring, he would take the piss. This meant that, unless Danny found Selwyn to be thoroughly interesting, he would be doing his usual thing. She could only hope that Selwyn was an interesting character.

Judith met them at the front door before they could ring the doorbell. She was wearing a flowery sarong, with her sun glasses perched high on her head, even though there had been no sign of any sunshine that day. She immediately hugged Theresa whilst giving her a big kiss on each of her cheeks.

'Are they new glasses?' she asked. 'They make you look intelligent and beautiful.'

'That's because she is intelligent and beautiful,' chipped in Danny.

'…and so are you, Danny,' she said and to Danny's horror, she gave him the same hug and kisses. 'We're 'round the back,' she said. 'Come on through.' As they walked through the house, Danny was busy wiping his cheeks dry.

Selwyn was sitting on the patio, smoking and he stood up to greet them. If first impressions are as important as it's claimed, he had already made a bad start. He was wearing bright red trousers, a rugby shirt and he had a thick cricket sweater draped around his shoulders. He was about Danny's age and had a receding hairline. Judith introduced him as Selwyn, but as he reached out his hand to Danny, he said 'Selwyn Forster – pleased to meet you both.' Theresa and Danny couldn't be sure if his name was actually "Forster" or whether he was really saying "Foster" in an upper class accent.

After clutching Danny's hand for far longer than was necessary, Selwyn turned to Theresa and proceeded to kiss her on both cheeks. Danny didn't approve of strangers kissing his wife.

'We're drinking Pimm's,' Judith announced.' Will you both have the same?'

Theresa accepted, but Danny pointed out that as he was driving, he ought to steer clear of alcohol. 'I've got some fresh lemonade in the 'fridge. Selly, darling, would you be a dear and fetch some for Danny while I see to Treese.' She didn't offer an alternative to Danny, but he was happy with lemonade.

"Selly" trudged off like an obedient collie while Theresa and Danny gave each other a little grin. Danny was wondering if he should tell Selwyn that you wear a sweater by pulling it over your head. It was possible that he had never learnt how to do it and would appreciate the gesture. Danny was going to enjoy himself after all. He decided to follow Selwyn to engage him in conversation. Theresa was glad about this because it gave her a chance to discreetly return Michael's key.

'Where is it you live?' Selwyn enquired of Danny as they walked to the kitchen.

'Woodnewton,' Danny replied, suspecting that Selwyn wouldn't have a clue where that was.

'How far is that?' Selwyn asked.

'About twenty five miles, I would guess,' Danny replied.

'Really?' was Selwyn's response, drawling the word out in his upper class accent.

'No, I thought I'd tell you a lie,' thought Danny who had an aversion to people who kept saying "really." Instead he asked 'Do you play?' while pointing to the cricket sweater.

'Say again?' Selwyn asked in return.

'Pardon?' asked Danny who knew what "say again" meant,

but he hated the expression, so decided to pretend to be ignorant.

'Say again … what was your question?'

'Oh, I was just asking if you played … cricket, I mean.'

'Fraid not,' was the reply. Danny knew a joke about a frayed knot, but this wasn't the time for it.

'You watch cricket, though, do you?' Danny asked.

'Very much, so,' Selwyn replied. That was another expression that Danny hated. Why say "very much so" when you can just as easily use a single word – "yes."

'Do you go to Lords?' Danny asked, because he recognised the colours as those of Middlesex.

'Good Lord, no. I watch it on the old plasma; the fifty inch jobbie – got the whole package, of course - movies; golf; cricket. What about you? Are you a cricket fan?'

Danny wasn't interested in playing competitions of material wealth. 'Yes, I usually watch the highlights in the evening,' he replied.

'Really?'

Danny was tempted to make some comment about Selwyn's rugby shirt, because he felt sure from his shape that Selwyn did not play, but as Danny had never been at all interested in the game, it might show up his own ignorance of the game.

Meanwhile, Theresa was busy talking to Judith. 'I hope you like Tapas,' Judith said. 'Selwyn likes to dabble in the kitchen, so he's got that all in hand.'

'Yes, we went to a little Tapas bar in Stamford a year or two back. It was very nice,' Theresa replied. She decided not to mention that Danny hadn't been very impressed.

'Selly has a time-share villa in Spain, so he's into everything Spanish,' Judith added. 'We're hoping to go there next month. How was sleepy old Norfolk? Did you get to work on your book?'

'Yes, I've made a good start and I picked up some good ideas while I was in Bircham.'

'You're not going to have a rape scene, are you?' Judith enquired.

'No, I'm not. I want to forget all about that, thank you, but some of the locals gave me some inspiration. That's all I'm saying at the moment.'

'Will you be going back sometime?' Judith asked.

'I'd like to, but only if Danny is able to join me. I don't want to stay there on my own again.'

Judith touched Theresa's arm and said 'No, of course not, dear. I quite understand. I was thinking of selling the place anyhow.'

'Why?'

'I don't get over there very often and it's not really giving me a very good return on my investment. Do you know that Selwyn could rent his little place in Hampstead for a sum that's more than the average UK wage? It's ridiculous, isn't it? But that's what property is like in London, these days.'

By now, the men were returning, so Theresa wanted to change the subject, but Judith had other ideas. 'I tell you what! Why don't you and Danny buy it off me?'

'What's this?' asked Danny, smiling because he thought he had just been scoring some useful points off of Selwyn.

'No!' said Theresa. 'Forget it!'

'Forget what?' insisted Danny.

Judith didn't grasp the reason for Theresa's determination. 'I'm thinking of selling *Cherry Tree Cottage* and I thought you both might like it.'

'No!' said Theresa, giving Judith a very hard stare. 'We already have a mortgage to pay off.'

'Well, we might consider it,' argued Danny. 'We're both earning decent money and the cottage would bring in some income. It might make a very good investment.'

'We'll discuss it in private,' insisted Theresa and gave Judith another hard stare. How could she have been so thick-skinned not to realise why Theresa couldn't consider such a scheme?

'Well, if you are interested, I'll let you have it for a very good price and we can both make a saving by not using an estate agent. You two have a talk about it. – no hurry.'

Theresa wanted time to come up with good reasons for her decision before discussing it with Danny. For now, she was determined to change the subject. 'What do you do, Selwyn?' she asked.

'I work with Judes – we're colleagues in the same department.'

As Theresa wasn't entirely sure what Judith did, that wasn't much help. Judith had told her once, but it hadn't registered and Theresa would feel foolish if she asked now. She knew it was something to do with legal affairs, because that was what she did when they had worked together nine years earlier. So that conversation died a death. Fortunately, after a few seconds silence, Danny came to the rescue.

'Nice car, Judith,' he said. 'Quite sporty I would think.' Danny had made the mistake of assuming the TT was her vehicle and the Evoque was Selwyn's, but he was wrong.

'Yes, I love it. The road-holding is remarkable,' she replied.

'It's the Quattro, isn't it?' Danny asked.

'No, that's mine,' Selwyn said. 'Jude has the Range Rover.'

'Oh!' said Danny feeling a little foolish. 'I just assumed that Judith would have the smaller car.' He nearly said 'the more girlie car,' but he stopped himself in time.

'What do you drive, Danny?' Selwyn asked.

'A Vectra,' Danny replied.

'I thought they'd stopped making them?' Selwyn added, trying a little one-upmanship.

But Danny wasn't going to take the bait. Instead he was

going to use reverse snobbery. 'They have. Mine's about seven year's old – very reliable and costs me very little to run.'

'Really?' The word lasted twice as long as it should.

'… And what's more,' continued Danny. 'We're a two car family. Theresa has a lovely little Ford Focus. She used to be a big fan of Datsuns, but it's been quite a while since she had her Cherry.'

Judith gave a little snort, which was her way of laughing. 'More than a while!' she said.

Theresa didn't mind a joke at her expense, but she still had to make a response. 'When Danny was young, he had ambitions to be a comedian. His parents weren't very happy about that. They said people would only laugh at him. They got that wrong.'

Selwyn wasn't laughing. The shared humour seemed to have completely passed over his head.

'Theresa is the lady I told you about who writes books,' Judith said to Selwyn.

'Really! I've never met a real life author before,' he replied. Danny wanted to ask if he's met any dead ones, but he was trying to behave himself.

'Do you read?' Theresa asked.

'Very much so.' Danny cringed again at Selwyn's repeated use of the phrase.

'What sort of things do you read?' Theresa was looking for another sale. Judith had previously declined a purchase as she said she never had time to read.

'I like fantasy things - with vampires and zombies, perhaps. Is that the sort of thing you write?' Selwyn asked.

'No, my work is more on the realistic side of things – nothing too heavy. So I can't tempt you into a purchase?'

'I'll take a rain-check if you don't mind. I've got enough books on my shelves that I never get around to read. Anyway – changing the subject - when shall I start preparing the food?'

Judith answered with a question 'Are we all hungry? I am. Shall we dine outdoors or is it too chilly? There is a cool breeze blowing off the river.'

Theresa was first to reply. 'It's not too bad now, but it will get cooler later as the sun goes down.'

'Let's start outside and re-locate for the later courses,' Judith responded.

'Courses?' questioned Danny.' How many courses are there?'

'I'm not sure, yet ...' Selwyn replied. 'Probably seven or eight. We'll see how we get on.'

'Good heavens,' said Danny. 'In that case, the sooner you start on it, the better. I have to go to work tomorrow.'

As they drove home, Theresa said 'Thanks for putting up with that. It can't have been much fun for you.'

'On the contrary,' Danny replied, 'I enjoyed it.'

'Really?' Theresa answered.

'Very much so,' Danny added and they both laughed. 'Yes, I thought Selwyn was priceless. He never seemed to grasp that I was making fun of him. Talk about thick-skinned! He kept that silly sweater wrapped around his shoulders all afternoon and all evening. I really felt like asking if he needed help putting it on properly.'

'What about the meal?' Theresa enquired.

'Well, on the whole it was tasty, but when we had Tapas that time with Tom and Shirley, we each ordered a couple of dishes and all tucked in. We didn't eat one dish at a time. That first course tonight – the Spanish sausage – was quite nice, but it needed something with it; like a salad or some rice. It was too spicy on its own. Then the next dish was a salad dish with some rice - and that needed something meaty – like a sausage, for instance. And so it went on. The garlic mushrooms needed something else; as did that cheese dish. Of course, I've never liked calamari and by the time the main dish arrived – that nice chicken – I was already quite full, but they both seemed to take it in their stride. No, on the whole, it wasn't a bad evening and it's good that you see your friends now and then,'

Theresa thought about this for a moment and said 'To be honest, I'm not sure I feel very close to Judith anymore. We used to be very good friends when we worked together, but she's turned into a bit of a yuppie. There was a time she would never have looked at someone like Selwyn … and why does she need a brand-new four-wheel drive vehicle? She gets the train to work every day – a waste of money, if you ask me.'

Danny responded 'Sometimes, people like to buy things for themselves that prove that they are doing all right. We've never thought like that. Mind you, I do think it's time I thought about changing this car. If I keep it much longer, I might have to start spending money on it.'

Theresa was glad to be talking about such trivial matters. She didn't want to explain to Danny why she was so against buying *Cherry Tree Cottage*, but she knew he would raise the subject at some point and she was still considering valid reasons why they should not consider it.

As they both sat down to their hot chocolate, Danny did bring up the subject again. 'I thought we could consider buying *Cherry Tree Cottage*, you know. We're well on top of our mortgage and we're able to put money aside for ISAs. We could look into another mortgage.'

'Hang on!' said Theresa, having had a little time to think about the subject. 'Your job isn't that secure at the moment. The last thing we need is for you to be out of work and then we have two mortgages to pay.'

Danny disagreed. 'I've been told that I will shortly transfer to another position. I can't guarantee that I will enjoy the new position, but at least I'll still have a job while I look around for something different.'

'While I was speaking to Judith,' Theresa said,' she told me the cottage hasn't been a very good investment. I think it's too far from the sea and it only has two bedrooms.'

Danny had an answer to that. 'That wouldn't matter. It's still bricks and mortar, so it's not going to lose money – and what rental we get will be a bonus.'

Theresa still had some more arguments to offer. 'What happens if we take out another mortgage and then the interest rates go up, like they used to do? We'd be in big trouble then. And … I've always thought we've outgrown this place. If we're going to borrow more money, I'd rather it was on our main home. You know I've always wanted a bigger garden. That driveway is a pain. If I leave the house before you, you have to move your car first – or sometimes vice versa. I'd love a bigger kitchen and a separate dining area.'

'Yes, that's true,' Danny responded.

'And it would be nice to have a patio so that we can have a proper barbecue outside.'

'All right; you've made your point. Perhaps, we should get this place valued and see what we can afford.'

Theresa was relieved that she had made some valid points. In any case, now that they were fully reconciled, it was time to think about their future.

Tess of the Dormobiles

Chapter 2 – "TOBY"

Tess drove the Dormobile onto the beach car park and as she turned off the engine, let out a huge sigh of relief. It had been a long tiring journey, having only stopped once for a light lunch at a service station. She had barely exceeded fifty miles per hour for the whole six hour journey. It wasn't that the vehicle couldn't travel faster than that, but Tess was still unfamiliar with it and there were so many fitments behind her that she didn't want to risk any emergency braking. She needn't have worried. The van was well screwed together, but trust would have to come with experience.

It was so peaceful now that the engine was switched off. She could just cook up a light meal in the back of the van, but she was too tired to tackle that – a task she would reserve for breakfast the next day. She had passed an inn a short stroll back beside the harbour. Tess was ready for a long drink and something substantial to eat, as well as the use of their facilities. She double-checked the car park sign and although it warned that vehicles were left at the owners' risk, it definitely didn't forbid overnight parking nor campervans. Moreover, it was free parking after six o'clock at night, but she realised that she would have to move on the next day. She drew the curtains to protect the contents from prying eyes and locked the doors.

Outside "The Fisherman's Arms," a noisy collection of drinkers was enjoying the warm summer evening and many of them allowed their gaze to wander as Tess approached the inn. She was used to this attention and she never tired of it. She was wearing her favourite turquoise jumper that hugged her well-proportioned chest and she deliberately tossed her long blonde hair so that the summer breeze caught it. Had she been wearing her high heels and a skirt, she knew she would have caused even more of a stir, but she was dressed in flat shoes for comfortable driving.

Tess paused at the doorway to study the menu posted in the window and was aware of more stares from behind, but she ignored them and carried on reading. She was hungry for some substantial fare, so she discounted the overpriced seafood options and decided upon a filling steak and ale pie.

Inside, there were two additional rooms leading off from the L-shaped bar. One appeared to be a modern extension and looked like the restaurant area. The other looked like a more utilitarian bar for serious drinkers and in earlier years would have been filled with smoke and darts players. Tess spotted a small table in the corner of the main bar area and decided this would suit her needs. 'Can I order some food?' she enquired of the smartly dressed young man behind the bar.

'Yes. Where will you be sitting?' Tess pointed to her chosen seat and ordered her pie.

'What would you like to drink?' the young man asked.

'I'd like a pint of your local ale, please. What do you recommend?'

'How about "The Fisherman's Friend?" We brew it ourselves.'

'It doesn't taste of menthol, does it?'

'No, no,' he replied with a polite smile. 'It's made with the best hops and barley.'

'That sounds fine. Can you put it on a tab?'

'It's quite a strong brew, that!' said a grey-haired, portly gentleman seated at the bar with his wife. 'Two pints of that and I'm anybody's!'

'Trouble is,' said his wife, 'that nobody wants him.'

'Well, you still seem to want me, my love!' he replied.

'Only for your pension! When I agreed to marry you, I should have looked at the small print – small being the operative word.' The barman gave a little snort of laughter.

'Are you on holiday, lass?' the husband asked, eager to change the subject.

'Yes, I've just arrived.'

'Where are you staying?' the woman asked.

'I'm in a campervan. It's parked on the beach for now, but I have to find somewhere else after tonight. Do you know of any campsites around here?'

The husband and wife looked at each other in thought. 'I don't think there's any in Burnham,' the wife said.

'Doesn't Toby live in a caravan?' the man asked of his wife.

'I believe he does. I don't know where, though,' the wife replied.

'Who's Toby?' asked Tess.

'A young lad who often comes in "The Fisherman's," said the man. 'He's got a fishing boat that he hires out for boat trips.'

'Will he be here tonight?'

'He might be. You can never tell with Toby – a bit of a free spirit, if you know what I mean.'

'If we see him,' said the woman, 'we'll give you a nod.'

'Thank you,' said Tess. 'If you would just excuse me, I'd better go and sit down before someone grabs my table.'

As Tess sat down, she felt that she may have sounded a little rude to have excused herself like that, but the inn was very busy and there certainly was a danger of her losing her table. She had also been struggling to hear the conversation due to another man standing beside her who insisted on talking in a very loud voice. She had often observed that some men do raise their voices as soon as they enter a bar and start drinking. She decided that she might offer to buy the couple a drink once she's eaten her meal. If she's to stay around here for a while, it would be handy to make a few friends.

While Tess waited for her meal to arrive, she let her eyes wander around the bar area. Apart from the annoying man with a loud voice, there was a cheerful atmosphere with lots of laughter, so typical of a harbour inn. She was still receiving occasional glances from various customers and when she returned them with a smile, the owners would quickly turn away, apart from one man seated at the next table, who let his stare linger a little longer than the others. His whole demeanour was in stark contrast to the jovial atmosphere in the bar. He wore a permanent scowl and his weaselly young male companion was also looking ill at ease with the world.

Tess felt her own mood change almost immediately. She had just realised that she was all alone in a strange place. Despite the cheerful atmosphere all around her, she knew none of these people. Supposing these men on the next table were violent criminals and they followed her back to the beach. She would be extremely vulnerable once everyone had returned to their homes. Her Dormobile was not going to be much of a safeguard against a determined felon. She had become used to being independent since the separation, but that was in a familiar town with her own home.

'Stop being so silly,' she told herself. 'You knew what you were doing when you embarked on this little trip.' She also told herself that she was tired and hungry after her long journey and she would feel better once she had some food inside her. A few minutes later her food arrived and she tucked into it with some relish. She soon forgot all her irrational misgivings and after only nine minutes, she was staring at an empty plate – actually two empty plates because the pie had arrived in its own dish with a good two inches of flaky pastry on top.

Tess sat back to enjoy her beer which she had been drinking cautiously after the warning of its strength, knowing she had been drinking on an empty stomach. She had developed the taste for good beer during her time as a student when all the other fellow graduates on her accountancy course had been male. Her ex-husband had not approved of her drinking beer, but he did have one sound piece of advice – it's always worth trying the local bitter as it usually made with more care and attention than the mass-produced varieties and beer doesn't always travel so well.

Tess' thoughts were disturbed as the man sitting next to her stood up and approached the bar to replenish his glass. As he did so, he glanced over towards Tess again, but she averted her gaze. While he stood at the bar waiting to be served, this gave Tess a chance to discreetly study him more closely. He was probably about five feet six inches tall, very thick-set with a beer belly that hung over his jeans. His long dark hair fell over his thick, short neck. As he returned to his seat, carrying two pints of beer, he looked at her. Tess could sense this and looked up tentatively. He gave a toothy grin and said 'All right?' He had a very dark stubbly chin. Whether this was from not shaving or whether he just had dark hair, she couldn't be sure, but she knew that she didn't want to get close enough to find out.

128

Tess muttered ungraciously 'Yes, thank you,' and wondered if she had done the right thing by responding, because he gave her the creeps.

To take her mind off of all this, she took out her mobile phone and sent a text to her father to let him know that she had arrived safely. He had tried to dissuade her from this little adventure, but Tess assured him that she could look after herself and to mollify him she told him she would text or phone regularly.

Just as she pressed "send," she was aware of some increased revelry as a tall man entered the bar. 'Toby!' she heard some people call out. So this was the Toby that the couple had talked about. Tess was impressed. He was tall and walked with an athletic gait. He was broad shouldered and narrow waisted, with sun-bleached hair that framed a face with strong features and a tantalising smile. Tess had already decided that she was going to steer clear of men for a while until the trauma of her divorce had subsided, but she was already reconsidering such a foolish idea. She knew nothing about this man, but she did have a good reason to talk to him. However, she would finish her ale and let him continue with his greetings to each of his many friends in the bar.

As she did so, she heard the "weasel" mutter to his friend. 'Bleeding Toby Thackeray – everyone's friend!'

'He's got his coming to him,' the dark stubbled man replied and then gazed towards Tess, wondering if she had heard, but Tess just carried on sipping her beer and looking at her 'phone. There was obviously some history between Toby and these two men. Without having a clue about that history, Tess knew whose side she would favour if it came to it, but she mustn't jump to conclusions.

She finished her beer, grabbed her bag and went up to the bar where the elderly couple were still seated. 'You probably realised that's Toby just come in,' said the woman.

'Yes, it was hard not to spot that,' Tess replied. 'Can I buy you both a drink?'

'That's very kind of you, love, but I'm driving and Jim's only allowed one drink.'

'What about a soft drink?' Tess asked.

'We don't do soft drinks, lass,' Jim replied.

'Perhaps another time, then,' Tess added. 'If I find a place to stay, I may be in here again. I'm Tess, by the way.'

'I'm Jim and she's Dotty,' said Jim with a mischievous smile.

'Dorothy!' said the lady. 'Although I was dotty when I married him!'

Just then, a man entered the bar and loudly announced 'I think your services are going to be required again, Toby. Someone's left a camper on the beach and the tide's come in over the door sills.'

A loud cheer went up in the bar and someone said 'That's another twenty five quid for your coffers.'

'Oh, God! That's probably me!' Tess exclaimed and rushed outside to see the evidence. As she ran down the road to the car park, she could see that the tide had risen dramatically since she had parked the van. A further vehicle had its wheels in the water, but that driver had parked slightly further up the beach and his vehicle could still be driven out. However, Tess' van was much deeper in the water and not only were the doors covered, but so was the exhaust, meaning she couldn't start the motor without risking water in the engine.

'Don't worry!' said a calming voice behind her. 'We'll soon have her out of there.' It was Toby. 'You're not the first to come unstuck here. The council ought to put up a sign to warn people. Their sign just says "Vehicles are left at the owners' own risk," so they think they've covered themselves.'

'What am I going to do?' Tess asked, trying not to sound like a silly hysterical woman.

'Just stay there a minute,' Toby said.

A few minutes later, he pulled up in an old beaten-up Land Rover Defender. He went round the back of his vehicle and donned some wellingtons. 'I'm going to winch it out,' he said and proceeded to attach his winch to the back of the campervan, taking up most of the slack with the winch. Tess watched his muscular forearms go to work and noticed his powerful back straining the grey teeshirt. This was a man used to hard work and something inside her was stirring. If her husband had looked like this, she might have made more of an effort to save their marriage.

130

'Is the handbrake on?' Toby asked.

'Yes, of course it is,' her mind distracted from the matter in hand.

'That's all right. Give me the keys. I'll go and take it off. Did you leave it in gear?'

'No, it's not in gear,' Tess replied.

Toby then waded into the water and released the handbrake. He returned to the Land Rover and operated the winch until the van was well out of the water. He applied the handbrake and released the winch. The camper was still on the beach car park, but safely out of harm's way.

'I don't know how I can ever thank you,' Tess said with relief written all over her face. Toby could think of a way, but he was too polite to say it.

'Don't mention it. Just don't do it again,' he said with a grin.

'I heard someone say something about another twenty five pounds. Is that some kind of a bet?'

'No, I often charge for this service.'

'Oh!' said Tess, disappointment showing on her face.

'But don't worry. I don't charge every time.'

'Why do you charge sometimes and not others?' Tess asked.

'It depends on whether the person in question has wound me up or not. We get a lot of city slickers come down here and think they can throw their weight around. They're usually the ones I charge. Last week, I charged one bloke fifty quid – a real dickhead!'

'Do you pay tax on that?' Tess asked with a smile.

'Hardly! I usually buy everyone in the pub a drink. Talking of which, I've got a half glass of beer going flat.'

'Can I buy you another?' Tess asked, wanting to show her gratitude, but also wanting to continue their conversation a little longer.

'No, thanks. I'm driving and I've already had one – at least, I will have done once I've finished my pint.'

'I wanted to ask you something, if you don't mind,' Tess said. 'I understand you live in a caravan.'

'That's right.'

'I hope to be around for a week or two. I don't think I can stay on this car park. Would there be any space where your caravan is parked?'

'It's not a proper camp site. It's a farm owned by a mate of mine. He lets me stay there as a favour. He might let you stay there. If you follow me back this evening, I'll have a word with him and you can see what you think.'

'Oh, that would be great if I could stay there. I'll pay some sort of rental. There's just one more thing. There were two men sitting near me in the bar. They don't seem to like you. I overheard the dark-haired one say something about you're going to get yours. I thought I ought to warn you what he said.'

Toby grinned. 'That will be Terry Parnell and his little mate Trigger. They're always looking for trouble. They've both enjoyed Her Majesty's Pleasure.'

Tess took a moment to work out what Toby meant. 'Prison?' she asked. 'What for?'

'Breaking and entering – and GBH. Parnell got upset with me over his girlfriend. She threw herself at me when he went inside. I wasn't interested. I tried to tell him, but he wouldn't believe me. Don't worry about him. He's a nasty bit of stuff, but I can deal with him.'

'Oh, well. I thought I'd better tell you anyway. By the way, my name is Tess.'

'Tess,' he muttered, and then thought about it for a moment. 'Tess! Of course … of the Dormobiles! Wasn't there a book written about you? By wothisname – Oliver Hardy?'

Tess smiled. She suspected that he was joking. 'Thomas, actually.'

'Of course … Oliver Thomas!'

And they both laughed as they walked back to "The Fisherman's Arms."

Chapter 15

It was suddenly autumn. One day there was the balmy sunny weather of late summer, albeit with chilly nights, and then September was erased by wind and a drop in daytime temperatures of ten degrees centigrade. For Theresa and Danny, it seemed that the birth of October had signalled a real return to the normality they craved - no more trips to Norfolk and their miserable separation firmly behind them both.

With the notion of relocating, they spent the next few weekends visiting the various attractive villages within reasonable commuting distance of Stamford and Peterborough. Together with the property pages from the 'Stamford Mercury' and the 'Peterborough Evening Telegraph,' they selected a handful of their preferred locations. The villages of Barnack, Ufford and Bainton would satisfy both of them equally in terms of commuting, but the wider area was blessed with attractive communities in the neighbouring counties of Rutland and Northamptonshire. Danny arranged to have their own property valued, but they decided that they would not make any further definite plans until nearer the following spring. By then, Danny might have a clearer picture of his job situation. Although he had been told his position was secure, he had also been informed that there was a possibility that this would involve a move to the head office in Norwich.

Then a bombshell hit them and all their plans had to be shelved. Theresa came home one evening to find Danny already changed and sitting in front of the television watching a tea-time quiz .He told her that he was on 'gardening leave' pending an investigation into an alleged sexual harassment incident. Theresa's recently restored trust in him was instantly thrown out of the window. She started to imagine all kinds of unsavoury actions he might have perpetrated and was ready to shout at him, but he seemed quite calm about the situation.

'It's all a load of nonsense,' he said, seeing the look of alarm on her face. 'Let me tell you the story before you get the wrong end of the stick. A little while ago, we had to construct some test data for one of our systems. We wanted to make it as realistic as possible using real people, but we weren't allowed to because of confidentiality issues, So what we did was to take some copies of real data and just changed all the names. So we had fictitious names such as Lydia Breadbin, Philippa Bucket, Eileen Dover, Lucy Lastic, Hugh Jarsse and so on. We even satisfied the company's equal opportunities and diversity policy by having two gay Scotsman called Ben Doon and Phil McCavity.'

Theresa was looking impatient while he was saying all this.

'I'm sure you get the idea,' he continued. 'Do you remember in "The Simpsons" when Bart 'phoned up Mo's Tavern and got him to say *"I'm looking for Amanda Huggenkiss"*? Anyway, we also had someone called Norma Snockers.'

At any other time, Theresa might have laughed at this, but she didn't even smile. Danny quickly carried on. 'As it happens, there is a woman who works there whose name is Norma … and she has … well, she's rather buxom.

'Yesterday, I went to the kitchen to make myself a drink and Norma was using the kettle. So I waited until she had finished. While the kettle was coming to the boil, she said she had to visit the ladies and that she would be back shortly; the inference being "Don't touch that kettle." Terry Bush came in and stood beside me and asked if the kettle was for my drink. I said "No, it's for Miss Snockers."

He looked a bit embarrassed and I realised that she was standing right behind me. I thought she was going to take longer in the ladies, but apparently, it was occupied. So she returned earlier than I expected. She glared at me and said "Right, I'm reporting you!" ... and she did.

'That afternoon, my manager summoned me and said Norma had accused me of making offensive remarks of a sexual nature. I told him what I'd said in the kitchen and that I would never had said it to her face ... and that I'd said "Miss Snockers" – not "Miss Knockers", which probably sounded the same to her.'

Theresa was angry. 'You never know when to stop trying to be funny, do you? I think I would have been offended if I thought someone was making disparaging remarks about my knockers.'

'But I didn't make disparaging remarks about her knockers. It was just a bit of office banter between me and Terry. I don't see why she should get upset enough to want to get me in trouble. If someone made a remark about my anatomy, I would just laugh it off. Unfortunately, Norma doesn't have a sense of humour.'

'I'm sure it will all blow over,' said Theresa with a sigh.

'Well, it would apart from two things I haven't told you.'

'And what are they?'

'Firstly, there is a strong rumour that she's having an affair with Des Troubridge - the HR director ... and he's a real nasty piece of work. He wields a lot of power in the company. Everyone is scared of him.'

'Trust you to pick on her, then. What's the other thing you haven't told me?'

'I'm already on a warning.'

'What! Whatever for?'

'I was overheard threatening to punch someone's lights out.'

Theresa couldn't believe her ears. She could believe Danny might make a stupid unguarded remark by way of his idea of humour, but she considered him far too sensible to

135

threaten someone with physical violence at work. 'Who was this you threatened?' she asked, her voice now quavering.

Danny looked at her and hesitated before replying. 'Michael Bingham.'

'Bloody Michael Bingham!' she shouted. 'Why does he keep plaguing our lives? Why did you threaten him, for Heaven's sake?'

Danny was now speaking in a soft voice, patently showing his shame at his impetuous actions. 'I had to visit the Norwich office just a few days after I went to live with dad. I hadn't been getting much sleep and I had a lot of anger in me. Michael wanted to go for a drink and a meal after work and I told him "no," but he kept pestering me. In the end, I just snapped and grabbed him by the lapels. After all, he was the one who had caused our separation.'

'And you threatened to punch his lights out!' added Theresa.

'Yes. I thought we were alone in the corridor, but one of the managers from Finance just happened to come out of his office and saw what was happening. I don't know this chap and he didn't know me. Naturally, I let go of Michael as soon as he appeared. He wanted to know what was going on. Michael, to his credit, told him we were just larking about, but the Finance chap obviously didn't believe him. He wanted to know who I was and I told him. Michael continued to make light of it all. He could charm the birds out of the trees when he wanted to, so the manager walked away. I thought that was it, but the next day, I was summoned to the HR Manager's office and I had to explain myself. It seems that he had already spoken to Michael. What Michael said I've no idea, but I was told that I could expect a written warning.

'Under the circumstances, I can consider myself lucky. It should really have been instant dismissal for gross misconduct. I was talking to dad about it and he said it reminded him of an instance back in the sixties when someone he worked with was given a week's notice for fighting in the factory, but it was rescinded when the union rep. argued that fighting was gross misconduct and it should have been instant dismissal, but because the foreman had given him a week's notice, the bloke got off on a technicality.'

Theresa just stared at him and muttered 'I can't believe you would have been so stupid.'

'Neither can I. I should have made sure no one was watching and then thumped him. Fancy getting caught like that!'

Theresa realised that this was Danny's way of making light of the matter, but she didn't feel like laughing. 'What happens next?' she asked.

'I don't really know. I suppose I just sit at home until I hear something. It seems to me that, these days, a bit of friendly banter is considered more unacceptable that threatening someone with physical violence. Look on the bright side. I'm on "gardening leave" so I'll get on with some gardening. I can paint that back fence before the weather gets too cold - and clean out the guttering.'

Ten days later, Danny was back at work. His manager had persuaded Norma to withdraw her complaint as long as Danny wrote a grovelling apology, which he duly agreed to. Danny suspected that he still had valuable knowledge that the company didn't want to lose – at least not until his KT was complete.

At least, the 'gardening leave' had resulted in their guttering being now clear of all moss and leaves, ready to cope with whatever autumn and winter could throw at their property which was now enhanced by a willow green fence. That might help when they came to sell their house.

Theresa was glad that she had decided not to tell Danny about Michael's advances to her. He had demonstrated that when riled, he could become violent. She was also very disappointed that he had kept all this from her, but as she also had her secrets regarding Michael Bingham, it would have been hypocritical of her to berate Danny for his lack of total honesty.

Tess of the Dormobiles

Chapter 3 – "A Quiet Night"

Tess was unable to sleep. She should have been totally exhausted after her long tiring day, but she usually struggled on the first night in a strange bed. She told herself that the following nights would be better once she was accustomed to the bed and the quiet surroundings, but that wasn't helping her now. For one thing, every time she closed her eyes, she saw vehicles coming towards her – hardly surprising after a six hour journey when such sights had been subconsciously etched on her mind. She was also re-living the events of the evening … mainly the embarrassment of getting the Dormobile stranded in the water and needing to be rescued. How could she have been so stupid? Still, that had helped break the ice with Toby. She would have still approached him about the farm site, but there was no guarantee that he would have helped a total stranger.

Then there was the sinister encounter with Terry Parnell and his weird little sidekick. That was enough to keep her awake on its own. She did hope that Toby was able to look after himself, because the two men were known villains. You seldom receive a prison sentence for a first offence, which meant they were either habitual criminals or their offence had been very serious. Either way, these two were certainly worth a wary eye.

When Tess and Toby had returned to the "Fisherman's," Toby politely excused himself saying that he had to see someone about a bit of business and he would see Tess later. She was rather disappointed about this as she wanted to find out a bit more about him, but she guessed that his 'business' was to do with his livelihood, so she knew this would have to take precedence. Tess re-joined Dorothy and Jim at the bar and they all got to know each other better.

Now, as Tess lay in her bed, she tried to remember some of their little witticisms. It was clear that, despite their bickering, there was a lot of love between them and Tess suspected that some of the little quips were tried and tested. 'Never go to bed on an argument!' Jim had said. 'Do you know, some nights we've sat up arguing for ages!'

'And what was that other one?' Tess asked herself. 'Oh, yes.'

'The secret of a good marriage is to eat out at least once a week – she has Mondays and I have Thursdays.'

This wasn't helping Tess to sleep. She picked up her book. Sometimes she found reading relaxed her mind and induced some sleepiness. She was currently reading a novel about William Marshall who was a great knight in medieval times. In fact, he was a driving force behind the Magna Carta. Tess was making up for her failure in history at school. She felt it was such a fascinating subject, but her teachers had made it all sound so boring, trying to ram dates into her when she was more interested in the characters themselves. Over the last few years, she had discovered Patrick O'Brian, Bernard Cornwell and now, Elizabeth Chadwick – great writers who brought history to life.

After twenty minutes of reading, her eyes were feeling the strain, so she turned off the light and tried once more to sleep. As she lay there, her mind went to Toby who was asleep in his own bed just a few yards away – or maybe he was lying awake thinking of her. She had enjoyed the little joke they had shared together. It wasn't actually that funny, but it did reveal something else – a little chemistry between them both. Or was that just wishful thinking?

Still no sleep!

She partially drew back one of the curtains. It had still been just about light when they had driven up to the farmyard. The farmer was happy for Tess to stay there for a couple of weeks, but he wouldn't accept any money. He said that if he started taking money, he would have to provide facilities and he didn't want to do that – nor accept responsibility for any problems. And now looking out over the farm, she could see his point, but the lack of facilities at least meant there were no other campers disturbing the calm night.

The moon was full and bright, and from Tess's limited knowledge of the tides, this explained the very high tide that had caught her out. The farm was washed in moonlight. A barn owl swooped silently past her window, taking her momentarily by surprise. She opened one of the side windows to let in some fresh air and listen to the silence and look at the stars. There were millions of them. You didn't see stars like this in the city where the light pollution washed out all but the brightest. It was light enough for her to see the time on her watch – two fifteen. Was she ever going to sleep?

Then her thoughts were interrupted by the sound of a car's engine. That was puzzling. The farmer hadn't gone out after she had met him and Toby's Land Rover was parked over by his caravan. It was getting louder, but she could see no lights. And then she saw it coming up the farm track; a dark shape with no lights. She kept her head down as much as she could while still looking out at the car. It pulled up near to Toby's caravan and two people got out. One of them went to the boot to fetch something. They had no idea that Tess was watching them. She recognised the shape of the man who had been driving. He was thick set with a beer belly. She was sure it was Terry Parnell. It may have been night-time, but the moon made it bright enough for her to see quite clearly; clearly enough for her to assume that the smaller man was the 'weasel.'

Tess realised that she was trembling. These two were up to mischief. She wished that she could alert Toby in some way. Then she spotted that the bigger man was carrying something - it was a petrol can. They were going to torch Toby's caravan while he slept! She had to do something. It was no good running out there and shouting. That would put herself in danger.

She climbed into the driving seat and started the engine. Turning on the lights and trying to sound the horn all at the same time, she wheeled the Dormobile around so that the lights were shining straight at the two men. She flicked the lights onto full beam to blind them and continued to sound the horn. She realised that she was driving in her bare feet and all she was wearing was a skimpy teeshirt and her knickers. Her heart was pounding as she stopped a few yards away from them. What did she do now? One of the back windows was still open and she heard a voice saying 'Shit! Let's get out of here.' The men were running back to the car just as Toby appeared at the caravan door. The car was started and they drove in reverse down the farm track, still with no lights. Tess heard a thump and realised that they had hit a gate post. After driving forward a few yards, they corrected their direction and continued reversing until they reached the road.

'Who was that?' Toby yelled.

'That was your two friends from the pub. Terry … Terry…'

'Parnell?' asked Toby, leaving his mouth wide open.

'… and they had a can of petrol in their hands.'

'My God! I wouldn't have stood a chance. You've saved my life. How can I ever repay you?'

Tess was shivering even more now – from both the shock of the events and also because she was wearing very little, but she managed a reply. 'I think the going rate is twenty five pounds, but I'll let you off as you didn't charge me.' It was still light enough to see his grin. 'Shouldn't we call the police?' she asked.

'There's no point. They won't do anything.'

'But I saw them … and recognised them.'

'Maybe you did, but it's late at night and no one would believe you could positively identify them. And after all, they didn't actually do anything. By now, they'll be back at home and have their alibis all sewn up. You're shivering,' he said. 'Is it cold in the van? God, what are you wearing?' He had suddenly realised that she wore very little and his eyes had now grown accustomed to the light and could see her bare legs.

'I didn't really have time to get dressed, did I?'

'No, I'm very glad you didn't.' He realised that his statement could have been misinterpreted. 'That is … you might have been too late. I didn't mean I'm glad you're not wearing very much. Let me get you my coat.'

'No, it's all right. I'll be fine once I get the van back across the farm track and get myself back in bed.'

Toby nodded; then said 'I could make some coffee to warm you up.'

'No, coffee is the last thing I need. I've been struggling to sleep as it is. I'd better get back. I'll see you tomorrow.'

'Are you going to be all right on your own?'

'Are you?' she asked. 'They won't come back, will they?'

'Not if they've any sense. In fact, by the time I've finished with them …' and he left the sentence hanging.

Chapter 16

It was now well into November and the clocks had been turned back, meaning Danny and Theresa had to face the commute home in the dark. Although their home in Woodnewton was a similar distance for both of their journeys, Danny was invariably the first to arrive back because in his current uncomfortable work situation, he would leave work bang on time, whereas Theresa was almost always too busy to do the same. Consequently, it befell Danny to make a start on their evening meal, so that Theresa usually found him busy in the kitchen.

But on one occasion, he abandoned his chores as soon as she walked through the door because he was anxious to talk to her.

'What's happened now?' she enquired sensing that something was amiss.

'It's our mate Michael, again,' Danny said, but he was smiling as he said it. 'He paid a visit to the Peterborough office last week. He kept out of my way, I'm pleased to say. You won't believe who he made a pass at!'

'Who? The Managing Director? The toilet cleaner? I don't know! Just tell me!'

'Norma!'

'What Norma Snockers?'

'The very same! He was booked in to stay at the LodgeHouse. You know, our company's version of a Travelodge or a Premier Inn - and he was wandering around the offices, looking for someone to share the evening with when he came across Norma at a photocopier. Apparently he started with the old patter; chatting her up and asking her where she lived and so on. Norma was polite and friendly in return and told him she lived in Ramsey. He didn't know where Ramsey is, so she explained that it's just south of Peterborough in the Fens. Then he asked her to join him for the evening. Everyone else, of course, knows she's seeing Des, but being from Norwich, he was unaware of that.

Michael thought he was onto a winner there, but she turned him down flat as you would expect. Michael, taken a bit by surprise said *"I hear there are lots of dykes in the Fens"*. As you can imagine, Norma took offence and slapped him on the face.'

'Oh, that's great,' said Theresa. 'I wish I'd have been there to see that. Did she lodge a complaint against him?'

'I don't think so,' replied Danny. 'She probably thought slapping him might have got her in trouble as well.'

'That's made my day,' Theresa said, gripping her fists together in glee.

'Of course, that's not all,' said Danny.

'There's more?' Theresa asked.

'Yes, but not so funny, I'm afraid. As he didn't have any success with Norma, he found someone else.'

'It was the toilet cleaner!' Theresa exclaimed.

'No. He was seen that evening, at the LodgeHouse with Muriel from HR.'

'I don't think I know her, do I?' Theresa asked.

'No, but she's married to Gerry from Marketing, who spends a lot of nights away on business.'

'A married woman!' Theresa said with disgust. 'I expect it of Michael, but she ought to be ashamed of herself.'

'Well, he does seem to have a way about him. You weren't tempted when you met him, were you?' Danny asked.

'No,' she replied. 'You know I don't go for good looking men!'

'Right!' Danny said. 'Just for that you can get your own meal,' and he pushed her onto the sofa. Theresa re-acted by jumping up and rushing Danny against the nearest armchair and they ended up on the floor in a heap, having a playful wrestle. This was not unusual and often served as a few minutes of foreplay and after rolling around for a few more seconds, Theresa found herself on top, mainly because Danny preferred her in that position.

Danny immediately grasped her buttocks and moaned with pleasure. Theresa could detect Danny's rising interest beneath her and was feeling quite amenable to letting him slate his hunger.

'Ooh, lovely bowling balls!' he said lustfully and the ardour he had generated in Theresa was killed instantly. The reference to bowling balls brought back all those unpleasant memories of her terrifying escapade with Michael and she stood up abruptly, leaving Danny feeling utterly frustrated on the floor.

'I'm hungry,' she muttered, heading for the kitchen.

Danny followed her and from behind, wrapped his arms around her waist whilst leaning his head on her shoulder.

'Bloody Michael Bingham!' she shouted. 'You know what I like about him?'

'No, tell me!'

'Nothing!'

Danny had decided that he would never again mention bowling balls. He assumed the fallout was because of his own history with Michael.

As they sat down to eat, Danny asked if Theresa wanted to look at any houses over the coming weekend.

'No, I have to go to Addenbrookes to see Elaine.' She replied.

'Who's Elaine?' Danny asked.

'Grandad's partner; girlfriend; whatever you want to call her. Mum called me to tell me that she's got cancer. I haven't seen her for a few months. I think I ought to go. You can come if you like?'

'No, thank you. I hate hospitals and I don't really know her. You know you can use the park and ride to get to Addenbrookes, don't you?'

'Yes, I did know.'

'Anyway, Danny added, 'it will only take half a day to do that. We've got the rest of the weekend.'

'And when am I supposed to do the housework?' she replied tetchily. 'I haven't touched my book for weeks. I just haven't got time to do everything.' Theresa desperately wanted to get back to her novel and develop the relationship between Tess and Toby.

Danny sighed. 'I thought you were the one who wanted to move house! Do you have to see this Elaine? She's not your relative.'

'I feel we owe her something for the fact that she brought a lot of happiness to Grandad's last few years.'

'But she stole your family's inheritance!'

'That's not fair! She didn't steal it. She sold her house to move in with Grandad and he wasn't going to leave her homeless when he died. Anyway, mum's not speaking to her, so the only way I can find out how she is, is to go and visit her – while I still have chance. I don't know how bad it is. Presumably, if she's in Addenbrookes, she must be having treatment.'

Theresa was feeling more and more frustrated with her writing and for several reasons. She had mentioned in the novel that there was some 'chemistry' between Toby and Tess, but had failed to illustrate it adequately. It wasn't enough to say there was chemistry. She had to involve the reader so that he or she felt it too.

She was also unhappy that Terry Parnell appeared as no more than a nasty villain. She wanted someone who oozed evil from every pore – like Bernard Cornwell had done with Obadiah Hakeswill in his Sharpe novels and brilliantly brought to life by Pete Postlethwaite in the television version, with his malevolent twitch and his bulging eyes.

But most of all, she was unhappy with the lack of progress in her writing. A professional writer should be writing at least a thousand words a day, but after several weeks, all she had for her efforts were three chapters. She had to face up to the fact that she would never be a professional writer unless she gave up her job as an architect and, in their current circumstances, that was not an option. Her sojourn to Norfolk had demonstrated that if she were to continue with her writing, it would be on a strictly amateur basis. Nevertheless, she would continue as and when time permitted. For one thing, she wanted to see how the story turned out and for another, she quite fancied Toby and was enjoying painting him in the image of the perfect lover.

When Theresa arrived at the hospital, afternoon visiting had already commenced and the wards were all busy. She eventually found the correct ward and could see that Elaine already had a lady visitor, so she wasn't sure if she should approach the bed, but Elaine spotted her and waved her in. 'I can come back a bit later, if I'm intruding,' Theresa said, noticing how frail and drawn Elaine looked.

'Of course, you're not,' Elaine said. You've come all this way to see me. I won't have you hanging around on my part. This is my daughter Grace. I don't think you will have met each other before.' Then she turned to Grace and added 'This is Theresa - Derek's granddaughter.' Theresa estimated Grace's age to be about sixty. Her eyes looked red as though she had been crying. Theresa could see the family resemblance.

They exchanged greetings and Theresa was offered a seat beside Elaine's bed. Theresa asked Elaine how she was.

'I'm not too bad at the moment. I have good and bad days.'

'It's bowel cancer, isn't it?' Theresa asked, based on her

understanding from her mother. 'They can treat that, I understand.'

'Well, it's a bit more than that, now. It's spread to several places. If they'd spotted the bowel cancer in time, they might have done something, but it's too late now. They've told me that if they give me some treatment, it will only add a few months to my life – if that – but I would be in and out of hospital. So we've agreed to leave it.'

Grace sobbed.

'I'm so sorry, Elaine,' Theresa whispered.

'I've had a good innings. I'm going to try and enjoy my last few days – at least as best I can with my health failing. I'm going home tomorrow. When things get too bad, I'll probably go into the nursing home at Thorpe Hall.'

'I'd like to come and visit you, there, if I may. Will you let me know when you go in?'

'That's very kind of you,' Elaine replied. 'Of course I will. Grace and I were just talking about your grandfather and I said I didn't have a photograph of him. Would you be able to lay your hands on one?'

'I'll see what I can do,' Theresa replied and then she had a brainwave. She reached into her handbag and took out a copy of her novel. 'How about this?'

Elaine took the book in her hand and saw the picture of Theresa's grandfather on the cover. 'It looks just like him. It *is* him! *Happy is a Grumpy Road* by Theresa Finbow. You wrote this?' she asked.

'Yes, I wrote it.'

'I didn't know you were a writer. Is it about Derek?'

'No, it's not about him, but he did inspire me to write it. I started writing it soon after he died. It's about an old boy who has turned into a bit of a grumpy old soul and has got himself into a bit of a rut since his devoted wife died. His family suggests that he tries a dating agency and he meets various ladies before meeting someone who eventually does bring him happiness.'

149

'Well, it *is* about him, then. It's exactly what happened to him.

'Yes, but I've added a lot of extra fictitious material – and the lady whom he ends up with is nothing like you. Will you take this as a gift?'

'You must let me pay for it,' Elaine responded.

'No, it's a gift. I didn't bring any flowers because so many hospitals these days don't allow flowers. So please take it – but you must promise to read it.'

I will, I promise – and Grace likes reading. I'll pass it on. In fact, I'll leave it to her in my will, she said with a mischievous glint in her eye. 'And I'll look forward to reading what you've said about Derek. He was a wonderful person. I can understand why you would write about him.'

Grace stood up. 'If you're going to start talking about him again, I'm going to have a break and a cup of tea,' she said.

'No, please don't go on my account,' said Theresa.

'No, really,' Grace responded, 'I need a break and a drink. I'd just about run out of things to say to mum. I'll be back in a little while. You two carry on without me.'

Elaine waited until Grace was out of earshot and said, 'I'm glad she's left us alone. I wanted to explain about your father's inheritance.'

'There's no need,' Theresa said. 'I quite understand why Grandad left you the house. Mum and Uncle Bob should have been more understanding about it.'

'I need to tell you the whole story,' Elaine said. 'You see when I sold my house, we both decided to get our will's amended at the same time. You know what Derek's said when he died, but it also said that if he survived me the proceeds from the sale of my house would go to my three children and the house – assuming we hadn't had to sell it to pay to go into a home – would still have gone to your mother and her brother. And, of course, with Derek going first, my money stayed with me.

Now my will stipulates that if I survive Derek and the house is still available, it will go to your mother and brother. There are some items in the house that I brought or have bought since, which will go to my family. I appreciate that your mother has had to wait a few years longer for it, but the house will be theirs. I think my family will get the worst of the bargain, because we've been spending some of my money, but there's still a good bit left.

We did have a couple of nice holidays out of it. We had a sort of honeymoon when I moved in with Derek.'

'You mean the three-week cruise around the Mediterranean?'

'Yes. We had to have a shared cabin on that cruise. That was the first time we'd slept together. I don't mean – well, you know – but we did actually share a bed. He said if I was expecting anything extra, he would have to get some Viagra. I told him that if he was going to get some of those, he'd better get something for me as well.'

Theresa smiled. It was just the sort of thing her grandfather would have said.

Elaine continued. 'He said that making love at his age was a bit like trying to hit a billiard ball with a piece of string.'

'I've heard him tell that joke before,' Theresa said. '... before he met you, I should add. He always made us laugh. I saw him once filling out his pools coupon. This was years ago when Nan was still alive. I asked him what he would do with a big win. He said in his deep grumpy voice *"I'd send your gran on a trip to Iceland. She wouldn't want to go, but it would be the best way to get some peace and quiet around here."* He didn't mean it, of course. He thought the world of her.'

'I know he did,' said Elaine, wistfully. 'I never tried to take her place, any more than Derek could really replace Keith, but I think we shared a good companionship. We had a lot in common at a time when we both needed a friend.'

Theresa was only half listening. Her eyes were upon a

stocky man sitting with his back towards them near the entrance to the ward. She was sure it was Billy. What on Earth was he doing there? That was a silly question. He was visiting a sick relative – perhaps his mother. But if Billy was there, that probably meant Michael might suddenly appear, too. No, it couldn't be Billy. What was happening in her life? She had to get a grip of herself. She was falling apart.

'Are you all right, Theresa?' Elaine asked.

'What? Oh, yes, I'm so sorry. I was listening, but I think there's someone over there that I know.'

'If you want to go and say hello, I don't mind.'

'No, I wouldn't dream of it,' Theresa replied. 'In any case, I'm not sure it is him.' She realised that Billy couldn't drive, so how would he get there? If it was him, he might well have come with Michael. Perhaps Michael was busy trying to find a parking space. The car park was always very busy. If Billy had come on his own, he would have caught a bus to King's Lynn; then a train to Cambridge; followed by a bus from the station. It was possible, but it was much more likely that he had a lift with Michael who would also want to see his mother. She had to stay calm and gather her thoughts. She took a deep breath and returned her attention to Elaine. 'Does Grace know about your will?' she asked.

'Oh, yes. She's known all along. I should have told your family, but your uncle was so rude to me, that I decided not to say anything.'

Ignoring Billy for a moment, Theresa replied 'Uncle Bob was unemployed at the time and had lots of financial problems. He was counting on the legacy, so it hit him quite badly when he heard the will. He's back on his feet now. Anyway, you could still live for ages yet.'

'I don't think so, my dear.' Elaine could see that Theresa was still glancing at the man. 'Are you sure you don't want to go and speak to him?'

'No, of course not. Have you seen him before today?'

'Yes, I think he was here yesterday.'

'Was he alone? Did he have, say, a brother with him?'

'No, I think he was on his own.' That made it unlikely that Billy would make the journey on his own two days running – or did it?

Just then, an orderly came in with a tray of water jugs to hand out to the patients. The man whom Theresa took to be Billy stood up and fetched an empty jug from his mother's bedside. Now Theresa could see that the man looked nothing like Billy. What was wrong with her? What was this obsession with Billy and Michael?

'It's all right,' Theresa mumbled. 'It's not him.'

'What a pity,' said Elaine, not realising the relief that had swept over Theresa.

A few minutes later, Grace returned and the conversation turned to the weather and other inconsequential small talk. Theresa had the feeling that she was intruding on the family grief, so she said she had better make a move before it got dark.

After a few more pleasantries, Theresa was on her way to the bus stop. She realised that she now felt very tense. She was conscious that she was looking all around to make sure there were no nasty characters about to molest her. She knew she was being silly, but she just wanted to get home as soon as possible.

She had to change buses at the bus station. She found the stop she needed and boarded her bus to the park and ride. Normally, she would have climbed to the upper deck, because she liked the better views attained from above, but this time she decided the lower deck was safer, even though it was quite crowded.

After alighting from the bus, she ran to her car, except that she had trouble finding it. Panic crept in and she ran up and down several aisles before she found it. Then fumbling in her bag, she had difficulty finding her keys, but eventually she was in her car and locked herself in. She sat there for a good five minutes before she felt ready to drive off.

Once at home, Theresa felt more relaxed in the comfort of her own home, but she was still a little bad-tempered with Danny. 'What have I done, now?' he demanded.

'It's not your fault,' she sighed. 'I'm a little upset after visiting Elaine. She's probably only a few months to live. It's so unfair.'

So once again, she had felt the need to lie to her husband. A marriage that for so long stood for honesty and trust was now grounded in deceit to keep it together. She couldn't explain her silly moment of panic without also relating her experiences with Michael Bloody Bingham. She wasn't sure what Danny would do if he knew, but she was sure he would do something.

Chapter 17

Danny looked across at Theresa who was watching television. He had found her attractive right from their first meeting. It hadn't been love at first sight, rather a feeling that had grown steadily throughout their first year as a couple. He had been introduced to her by a friend anxious to make him move on from Susan. At the time, Danny had felt that Susan was the love of his life and no one would ever take her place. Theresa was different in so many ways. Both ladies were good looking, but Susan's looks were more about glamour. She was blonde for a start and she had the classic hourglass figure, but she lived life on the edge and that was too much for Danny. When she tried to entice him with some funny cigarettes, he didn't just decline. He got angry with her and told her about an old school friend who had started out smoking weed, but it had totally changed his character and Danny had vowed never to succumb. That had counted for nothing with Susan and she told Danny if he didn't like it, he could "naff off." So he did. But he then spent several months trying to contact her to seek a reconciliation, all to no avail.

Over the next few months, he dated two other girls, but they couldn't replace his feelings for Susan. Ronni and June were both fair-haired, so Theresa's darker hair at least made her different. She was more sophisticated than the others. In fact, Danny soon realised that she was more sophisticated than him, even though she was five years younger. She wore spectacles, but this only increased her attractiveness. Somehow the glasses served to frame her lovely high cheeks and deep brown eyes. However, her greatest appeal was her sense of humour and her delightful laugh. When, on their first date, she laughed at a couple of Danny's little off the cuff witticisms, it encouraged him to more and when Danny was in the right mood to tell jokes, his inventiveness for quick fire humour went into overdrive and they both ended up enjoying their first date enormously. Even so, Danny continued to hold a torch for Susan and it was a good nine months before he realised how much Theresa had come to mean to him.

What turned the corner for him was when Theresa went away for a week's holiday with her parents. After eight days without her, he greeted her with those magic three words – 'I've missed you. God, how I've missed you!' A few months later, he asked if they should get married; not exactly the most romantic of proposals – just a matter of fact question 'Should we get married?' Theresa agreed. As she was still studying for her architects qualification (although by now gaining work experience), she welcomed the security that marrying Danny offered her. Danny, at that time, had a secure position with Wilkinsons.

Since that time, their love for each other had deepened and their recent separation had caused both of them considerable heartache. Now, as Danny looked at Theresa, he hoped all that was behind them, but recently she was prone to admonishing him about trivial matters, which had never been the case before. What's more, he now had something else to tell her that would probably incur another admonishment.

'I have to go over to Norwich next week,' he said quietly.

'All right,' Theresa said, trying to concentrate on her television programme.

'And I'll be staying overnight,' he added.

'I thought you told me that you were never going to do that again,' she exclaimed, turning to give him a hard stare.

'I can't help it. We're doing a software upgrade at the same time as upgrading some servers. The new servers are going to be in the Norwich Data Centre.'

'But you don't support the servers, do you?' she asked.

'No, but I do support the software and I have to be "on call" if there's a problem. I wanted them to do the servers as a separate operation, but our wonderful Change Management Team insists that we keep the downtime to a minimum. If we did the two tasks separately, we would have to take the servers down twice, so they insist we do it all at the same time. The trouble is that if there is some kind of a problem, we won't know if it's the software or the servers, but my voice doesn't count for anything. Most of the members of these committees haven't got a clue what goes on. Some of them probably don't know what a server is!'

'Can't one of the Indians go instead of you? I thought you'd passed on your knowledge to them?'

'Unfortunately, the one with the best knowledge has gone back to India to support the system from there.'

'How's that going to work, then?' Theresa enquired.

Danny thought she was taking this all to heart. 'If you're worried about Michael Bloody Bingham, he won't be anywhere near where I'm going. I'm going to the Data Centre, which is a completely different building on the outskirts of town.'

Theresa let out an 'harrumph' and went back to her programme, but she could no longer concentrate. Michael Bloody Bingham's name had cropped up again. 'Let's go for a drink down the *Swan*,' she suggested.

'It's a bit cold out there,' Danny replied, taken a bit off guard. Theresa seldom made such a suggestion.

'Which means they'll have a fire going. We can wrap up and walk briskly. Come on! I'm going anyway.' That left Danny with little choice, because he wasn't going to let his wife wander out at night on her own and she knew it. Theresa was not subtle about getting her own way.

A week later, Danny duly made his way to the Norwich Data Centre. The upgrades were due to be performed at 2.00 a.m.

the following morning. Most organisations would have performed such an operation at the weekend, but WBH's business dictated that weekends were their busiest times, so they had to select a downtime that caused the least disruption to their business. Danny was expecting to do a lot of sitting around, doing nothing, so he left home at a leisurely mid-morning time to allow all the rush hour traffic to die down and avoid the notorious bottlenecks on the A47. On the way, he stopped to pick up a newspaper and a magazine, so he had something to read and a couple of crosswords to keep him occupied. If everything went according to plan, he would not be required to do any work at all, at least not until the following morning when the pubs started using the tills again. The software had been thoroughly tested, but nothing could ever be taken for granted,

Theresa meanwhile, was in a bad mood, especially as the traffic into Stamford was even worse than usual. A problem on the A1 had meant that a lot of drivers had ignored the diversion signs and sought a way through the town. She turned off on the Barnack Road, only to discover many other people had the same idea and her eventual parking spot left her a near half mile walk into town. She blamed Michael Bingham for that as well. As she walked to work, she was thinking about the grilling she was going to give to Danny the next day. She also made plans to cook a special meal for his return – just to show that she had missed him, which she knew she would.

So when she did enter the house the following day, she was ready to question him, but Danny sat on the settee looking very pale.' Are you all right?' she asked, forgetting about the grilling.

'Michael's dead!' Danny replied.

'What? How?' Theresa asked with trepidation.

'There was a fight.' Theresa's immediate fear was that

Danny had killed him, but Danny continued. 'Carl's been arrested. I've been at the police station all morning, answering questions.'

She sat down beside him and held his hand. She could tell that he was deeply upset. 'Why you?'

'I was there when it happened.'

'Where … why?' Theresa wanted answers, but Danny seemed a bit too shell-shocked to speak more than a few words at a time.

'Can I just have drink and then I'll tell you the whole story.'

'Of course … shall I make a cup of tea?' A cup of tea is always the best answer in moments of stress.

With a cup of tea in front of him, Danny related the story.

'I was just finishing my evening meal at *The Green Man* – the pub next to the LodgeHouse. I heard a voice say "*That's Tess' husband*," and then another voice, which I recognised as Michael's said "*Keep your voice down*." I looked up and could see a chap looking in my direction. It was, of course, Carl, but I didn't recognise him with his glasses. Michael was sitting opposite with his back to me.

Anyway, Carl ignored Michael and came over to ask if they could join me. I didn't want to be rude to Carl who'd never done me any harm, but I pointed out that I was just about to go. He wanted to know how you were – said he hadn't seen you in the village lately and wanted to know how the writing was going. He sat down and Michael sheepishly joined us.'

'Why were they there?' Theresa asked, thinking this all sounded a bit fishy.

'Carl was staying with Michael that night. He'd just been after a job on a farm nearby and didn't fancy going home on his bike at night. Michael always uses one of our pubs when he can – company loyalty or something. It really was just a coincidence them being there.

159

'Anyway, we carried on talking, with Michael playing little part in the conversation, which was unusual for him. By the way, you seemed to have made quite an impression on Carl. He wanted to talk about you all the time, which seemed to annoy Michael.

'Suddenly, out of the blue, Carl said to Michael *"How did you know the staircase had a dog-leg? You were there that night Lynn died. You were staying at ours that night. You killed her, didn't you?"*

'This seemed to be a continuation of an earlier conversation before they joined me and something had just triggered a thought in Carl's mind. Michael looked all flustered and said *"No, she tripped and banged her head on the beam. I couldn't stop her."* By now, Carl was getting redder and redder and you could tell he was about to explode. He was trying to contain his anger. *"But you were there, pursuing her, weren't you? You bastard!"* And then he lunged at Michael, grabbing him by the collar and wrestling him to the ground.

'It didn't take long for the management to eject them both and me as well, as I was in the same group, trying to stop Carl. It wasn't easy separating Carl. He was going wild. I told you he had reputation for a bit of a temper. Well, I saw it for myself.

'Outside, it all kicked off again in the car park. Punches were thrown. I tried to intervene, as you can see.' Danny turned his head to show a bruise on his cheek. Theresa hadn't noticed it before because Danny had been sitting with his other side to her. 'And my ribs are badly bruised,' he added.

Theresa clutched his hand tighter and smoothed his hair.

'Anyway, one punch sent Michael flying and he smashed his head against a concrete bollard. I could tell straight away that it was serious. He stopped moving instantly. Someone called an ambulance and the police turned up … and that was it really. The police started asking everyone questions and Carl was taken into custody.'

'Did he at any time say something like *"I'm gonna kill you!"* do you remember?' Theresa asked.

'I don't think so,' Danny replied.

'Well, that's something. If he had, that would go against him in court. As it is, he'll probably be charged with manslaughter. His poor wife! How will she take the news? He may have been a bit of scum, but she's lost a husband – and the children have lost their father.'

Danny nodded and added '... and then there's Michael's parents. How does it feel to know your son has died in a fight with his brother? How will they react to Carl?'

Theresa said 'I got the feeling that Michael was the blue-eyed boy with his mother, but his father isn't really his father. Billy found his birth certificate and saw a different name as his father.'

'I've never seen anyone die in front of me before,' Danny said, seemingly unaware of what Theresa had just said. 'One minute he was alive and kicking – literally – and then his life was snuffed out in an instant ... no more Michael ... just a body.'

Danny still looked washed out. Talking had taken even more out of him. Theresa asked 'Have you eaten?'

'Not really. I stopped on the way home for a burger, but I didn't eat it all. My mouth was too dry to swallow properly. My stomach feels all knotted up.'

'I know what you'll eat,' Theresa announced. 'I made a delicious Indian meal with a lovely creamy rich sauce. You'll find that easy to swallow. It just needs heating up in the microwave. I wanted something special for you when you came home. Will you open a bottle of wine to go with it?'

Theresa felt a little guilty that she was not too upset about Michael's death. She did feel for his family and particularly Billy, but the news had lifted a great weight from her mind. She could go back to Norfolk without fearing Michael suddenly appearing at her door. She could see that Danny had been shaken by the event, but a good meal and an early night would soon restore him. She might now be able to tell him about Michael's attack on her. It pained her that she had kept a big secret from him – but she wouldn't tell him just yet. He had enough on his mind.

As Theresa ventured into the kitchen to prepare their meal, she felt like humming a song, but she resisted the urge. She did consider that it was a coincidence that the place where Michael met his demise was *The Green Man* - a subject she had been researching for her book. It would have been even more ironic if he had been mown down by a Dormobile.

As she placed the meal in front of Danny, she told him to have a good swig of the wine which would act as an aperitif and prepare his taste buds for the curry. He still wasn't sure if he wanted to eat anything, but after the wine hit his palette and the aromatic spices wafted up, he tentatively took a mouthful and declared the meal to be the best Indian meal he'd ever tasted.

When they had an early night, Theresa initiated proceedings and Danny soon rose to the occasion, especially as Theresa took the dominant role. Afterwards, Danny accused Theresa of "giving him a good rogering."

'I don't think a woman can give a man a "rogering" unless she has that operation,' said Theresa '… a strapadictomy!'

'Whatever,' Danny murmured. He was too tired to argue or laugh at her little joke. He then fell into a very deep sleep and didn't wake up until after Theresa had left for work the next day.

Epilogue

As Danny parked the car outside *Cherry Tree Cottage*, Theresa called in next-door to get the key from Mrs Fitheridge. It was mid-May; between bank holidays and the first time that Theresa had been back to Bircham St. Mary's since September. 'Hello my dear,' Mrs Fitheridge said. 'I've only just finished cleaning the place. The previous tenants had left it in a terrible state. They even stole three of the light bulbs – those expensive hallucinogenic ones. I'll tell Judith to make sure they never come back. I know you always leave it nice and clean. I hardly have to do anything after you leave. Have you come to do some more writing, dear?'

Mrs Fitheridge was a friendly soul, but she did tend to go on a bit. She was also inclined to try and use big words, but often got them wrong. 'I hope to do some writing, but Danny is with me this time, so it's more of a holiday,' Theresa replied while Mrs Fitheridge took a breath.

'Well, I hope you have a wonderful time. If there's anything you need, you know where to find me. Don't hesitate to call. If there's no reply, I might be round the back, so have a look in the back garden – unless it's at night. It will be too dark then' and she gave her funny little laugh. 'There's a letter arrived for you. I left it on the kitchen table. It confused me at first because it said "Tess Finbow." I knew your "nom de guerre" was Finbow and I saw the booking was for Theresa Whitehead, but who else would have a letter sent care of *Cherry Tree Cottage*? I left some milk in the fridge for you.'

Theresa was wondering who might send her a letter at this address. 'It must be Millie!' she said, thinking out loud.

'Oh, that poor woman,' Mrs Fitheridge said … 'lost her husband last month.'

'Eddie? Eddie's dead?'

'Yes, he had a heart attack. It was in the pub. He was telling one of his little jokes. What was it now? Where do … no, wait a minute. What do you call people born in Norfolk … babies! He was busy laughing at his own joke as he often did and he was drinking his beer at the same time and some of it went down the wrong way. He starting choking and coughing and couldn't get his breath. He stood up to open his airways or something … and then … he just keeled over – had a massive heart attack. Les tried to give him artificial insemination, but it was no good and when the paraplegics arrived, he was dead.'

'Were you there when it happened?' Theresa asked, as she thought Mrs Fitheridge seemed to know all the details.

'No … someone told me what happened.'

'Poor Millie,' Theresa said … 'and poor Eddie. I liked him. I know he was a grumpy old bigot, but he was funny. I'll have to pay her a visit. Her address will probably be on the letter.' That was another sad death, she thought to herself. It had only been a few weeks since Elaine had passed away. Theresa had visited her in her last few days at Thorpe Hall. She looked a shadow of the person she had seen at Addenbrookes, but Theresa knew she was being well cared for. In memory, Theresa had donated a small sum of money to the Sue Ryder Organisation who administers Thorpe Hall.

Danny arrived and could see the two ladies talking. He was impatient to enter the cottage and have a cup of tea. 'Have you got the key, Theresa?' he asked.

'Oh,' said Mrs Fitheridge. 'I'll just get it for you.'

While she was doing that, Theresa mentioned Eddie's death to Danny. 'Who's that?' he asked.

'That was the old boy we met in the pub when you last visited … sat at the bar with Millie.'

'Oh yes, I remember,' Danny said.

Mrs Fitheridge re-appeared and handed the key to Danny.

'Yes, I always said he should have got more exercise. He only lived a few hundred yards down the road, but he made Millie drive him to the pub every night. She sometimes had to drop him right at the door while she parked the car. I love my walking … the best exercise you can get. And then, of course, we had another death a few months ago – young chap killed his brother.'

'Oh, you mean Billy?' Theresa said.

'Yes. You knew him then, did you? He had a terrible temper. To talk to him on the street, you wouldn't think him capable - perfectly harmless - but when he was riled – stand clear! He got two years for that. Of course, he's already served a few months on demand.'

Theresa hadn't realised that the case had gone to court and this was the first she had heard of the sentence. 'Two years seems a bit harsh,' she said. 'I thought it was just manslaughter. He didn't mean to kill him.'

'Aah, but he had previous.'

'Had he? I didn't know that.'

'Yes, he was on a suspended sentence for an incident in King's Lynn … a few years ago, it was now. He accused two local lads of trying to chat up young Lynn and he went for them like a maniac … injured a bouncer, as well. He didn't ask for bail, as he didn't want to go home so soon after … well, you know. It would have been uncomfortable for his mother.'

Danny took the key from Mrs Fitheridge's hand and without saying anything, went to the cottage. Theresa noticed that he was looking rather morose. For the first few months after Michael's death, he had been rather depressed, but had recently perked up and was eagerly looking forward to this break. Now, the mention of Billy seemed to have brought back all those bad memories. Theresa would have to use her charm on him to restore him back to the old Danny. She excused herself from Mrs Fitheridge and joined him at the cottage.

'If you take the cases upstairs, I'll make a cup of tea,' Theresa said.

While the kettle was boiling, she picked up the letter on the kitchen table. It was a plain brown envelope and the writing was a bit scratchy. She noticed that it was stamped. Surely Millie would have delivered it by hand. She opened it and looked at the signature. It said "Carl Bingham." Why on Earth was Billy writing to her? It read –

Dear Tess,

I do hope this letter reaches you. I didn't know your home address. I wanted to write to thank you for your kindness in talking to me. I took your advice about wearing my spectacles and as a result, I seemed to have re-gained a certain amount of self-confidence, which is quite important in this place. Show any sign of weakness and you could be in big trouble. My family do not want to see me at the moment, so I've had no visitors or any letters. I hope you don't mind me writing, but it helps to know I've communicated with someone. I'm trying to keep my nose clean so I get an early release.

I've also taken your advice about learning a trade, but it's in here rather than at the CITB place. I'm learning to be an electrician. I figure that with a criminal record, it will be hard to get a job when I come out, so I thought if I learnt a trade, I can set up my own business. People are always looking for electricians. I don't really know what the future holds, but at least I'm doing something while I'm here.

You must tell Danny that he mustn't blame himself for what happened. It was perfectly understandable and he had more to lose than me. So tell him to enjoy the rest of his life with my blessing.

Theresa stopped reading. This didn't make sense. Why would Danny be blaming himself? Perhaps Billy wasn't used to writing and yet ... he had made a decent job of it. His grammar was perfectly acceptable for a farm worker. She read the last paragraph again. It could only mean one thing but she didn't want to believe it and her knees buckled under the realisation. She sat down and held her hand over her mouth just as Danny returned.

'What's up?' he asked.

'You killed Michael!' she said in a croaked voice.

Michael didn't answer but took the letter from her hand. He sat down beside her. 'He said he wouldn't say anything to anyone. He obviously thought I would tell you.'

'You've been lying to me,' she said, her voice trembling with anger.

'No, I didn't lie. I just didn't tell you the whole truth. I said Carl attacked Michael – and he did. I said a punch was thrown – there was ... but it was mine. I struck the last punch – the one that ended it.'

'Why?' Theresa asked.

'I think you know why,' he replied. After a few more seconds, he added. 'While I was trying to prevent Carl attacking Michael, he said *"You'd want to hit him if you knew what he's done to your wife."* I said *"What did he do?"* Carl said he tried to have sex with you. I was so angry that I just struck out ... just one single punch. It caught him off guard and he fell. I didn't hit him that hard, but it was the way he fell. You talk about me lying to you. You never told me what he did.'

'No. Because I knew how you would react. I didn't want you to get into trouble. So you let Billy take the blame!'

'It was his idea. He thought if I got into trouble, I had more to lose. I protested, of course and when the police started talking to Carl, I just went along with it. I didn't think he'd get two years. I didn't think he would get sent to prison at all. I didn't know about his previous conviction until just now. If I'd known I wouldn't have let him take the blame. I feel terrible.'

Theresa looked him full in the face. 'Well, there's no point in doing anything about it now. By the time our justice system sorts it out, Billy will be out of prison. In any case, you would probably both be convicted of perverting the cause of justice, so it's too late now. The damage is done. It was very noble of Billy to take the blame.'

Danny nodded. 'He told me that he wanted the chance to speak in court about what a dreadful person his brother was. He didn't think his family would believe him otherwise, but he's paid the price.'

Theresa held Danny close to her and he responded likewise. 'I think it's time for us to both move on … no more secrets. We've got an extra responsibility now. In a few more months we're going to be parents – almost nine months since Michael's death.'

Danny said 'If it's a boy, I think we should call him Roger!'

Theresa pulled a face. 'That's a dreadful na… Aah, yes. I get it.'

Yes, it was time to move on, but there was one more secret they would each keep. They would never tell their child that his or her father was a killer.

Printed in Great Britain
by Amazon